The Agony Column

by Earl Derr Biggers

Originally published: 1916

CHAPTER I

London that historic summer was almost unbearably hot. It seems, looking back, as though the big baking city in those days was meant to serve as an anteroom of torture--an inadequate bit of preparation for the hell that was soon to break in the guise of the Great War. About the soda-water bar in the drug store near the Hotel Cecil many American tourists found solace in the sirups and creams of home. Through the open windows of the Piccadilly tea shops you might catch glimpses of the English consuming quarts of hot tea in order to become cool. It is a paradox they swear by.

About nine o'clock on the morning of Friday, July twenty-fourth, in that memorable year nineteen hundred and fourteen, Geoffrey West left his apartments in Adelphi Terrace and set out for breakfast at the Canton. He had found the breakfast room of that dignified hotel the coolest in London, and through some miracle, for the season had passed, strawberries might still be had there. As he took his way through the crowded Strand, surrounded on all sides by honest British faces wet with honest British perspiration he thought longingly of his rooms in Washington Square, New York. For West, despite the English sound of that Geoffrey, was as American as Kansas, his native state, and only pressing business was at that moment holding him in England, far from the country that glowed unusually rosy because of its remoteness.

At the Carlton news stand West bought two

morning papers--the Times for study and the Mail for entertainment and then passed on into the restaurant. His waiter--a tall soldierly Prussian, more blond than West himself--saw him coming and, with a nod and a mechanical German smile, set out for the plate of strawberries which he knew would be the first thing desired by the American. West seated himself at his usual table and, spreading out the Daily Mail, sought his favorite column. The first item in that column brought a delighted smile to his face:

"The one who calls me Dearest is not genuine or they would write to me."

Any one at all familiar with English journalism will recognize at once what department it was that appealed most to West. During his three weeks in London he had been following, with the keenest joy, the daily grist of Personal Notices in the Mail. This string of intimate messages, popularly known as the Agony Column, has long been an honored institution in the English press. In the days of Sherlock Holmes it was in the Times that it flourished, and many a criminal was tracked to earth after he had inserted some alluring mysterious message in it. Later the Telegraph gave it room; but, with the advent of halfpenny journalism, the simple souls moved en masse to the Mail.

Tragedy and comedy mingle in the Agony Column. Erring ones are urged to return for forgiveness; unwelcome suitors are warned that "Father has warrant prepared; fly, Dearest One!" Loves that would shame by their ardor Abelard and Heloise are frankly published--at ten cents a word--for all the town to smile at. The gentleman in the brown derby states with fervor that the blonde governess who got off the tram at Shepherd's Bush has quite won his heart. Will she permit his addresses? Answer; this department. For three weeks West had found this sort of thing delicious reading. Best of all, he could detect in these messages nothing that was not open and innocent. At their worst they were merely an effort to side-step old Lady Convention; this inclination was so rare in the British, he felt it should be encouraged. Besides, he was inordinately fond of mystery and romance, and these engaging twins hovered always about that column.

So, while waiting for his strawberries, he smiled over the ungrammatical outburst of the young lady who had come to doubt the genuineness of him who called her Dearest. He passed on to the second item of the morning. Spoke one whose heart had been completely conquered:

MY LADY sleeps. She of raven tresses. Corner seat from Victoria, Wednesday night. Carried program. Gentleman answering inquiry desires acquaintance. Reply here. --LE ROI.

West made a mental note to watch for the reply of raven tresses. The next message proved to be one of Aye's lyrics--now almost a daily feature of the column:

DEAREST: Tender loving wishes to my dear one. Only to be with you now and always. None "fairer in my eyes." Your name is music to me. I love you more than life itself, my own beautiful darling, my proud sweetheart, my joy, my all! Jealous of everybody. Kiss your dear hands for me. Love you only. Thine ever. --AYE.

Which, reflected West, was generous of Aye--at ten cents a word --and in striking contrast to the penurious lover who wrote, farther along in the column:

--loveu dearly; wantocu; longing; missu -

But those extremely personal notices ran not alone to love. Mystery, too, was present, especially in the aquatic utterance:

DEFIANT MERMAID: Not mine. Alligators bitingu now. 'Tis well; delighted. --FIRST FISH.

And the rather sanguinary suggestion:

DE Box: First round; tooth gone. Finale. You will FORGET ME NOT.

At this point West's strawberries arrived and even the Agony Column could not hold his interest. When the last red berry was eaten he turned back to read:

WATERLOO: Wed. 11:53 train. Lady who left in taxi and waved, care to know gent, gray coat? -- SINCERE.

Also the more dignified request put forward in:

GREAT CENTRAL: Gentleman who saw lady in bonnet 9 Monday morning in Great Central Hotel lift would greatly value opportunity of obtaining introduction.

This exhausted the joys of the Agony Column for the day, and West, like the solid citizen he really was, took up the Times to discover what might be the morning's news. A great deal of space was given to the appointment of a new principal for Dulwich College. The affairs of the heart, in which that charming creature, Gabrielle Ray, was at the moment involved, likewise claimed attention. And in a quite unimportant corner, in a most unimportant manner, it was related that Austria had sent an ultimatum to Serbia. West had read part way through this stupid little piece of news, when suddenly the Thunderer and all its works became an uninteresting blur.

A girl stood just inside the door of the Carlton breakfast room.

Yes; he should have pondered that despatch from Vienna. But such a girl! It adds nothing at all to say that her hair was a dull sort of gold; her eyes violet. Many girls have been similarly blessed. It was her manner; the sweet way she looked with those violet eyes through a battalion of head waiters and resplendent managers; her air of being at home here in the Carlton or anywhere else that fate might drop her down. Unquestionably she came from oversea-- from the States.

She stepped forward into the restaurant. And now

slipped also into view, as part of the background for her, a middle-aged man, who wore the conventional black of the statesman. He, too, bore the American label unmistakably. Nearer and nearer to West she drew, and he saw that in her hand she carried a copy of the Daily Mail.

West's waiter was a master of the art of suggesting that no table in the room was worth sitting at save that at which he held ready a chair. Thus he lured the girl and her companion to repose not five feet from where West sat. This accomplished, he whipped out his order book, and stood with pencil poised, like a reporter in an American play.

"The strawberries are delicious," he said in honeyed tones.

The man looked at the girl, a question in his eyes.

"Not for me, dad," she said. "I hate them! Grapefruit, please."

As the waiter hurried past, West hailed him. He spoke in loud defiant tones.

"Another plate of the strawberries!" he commanded. "They are better than ever to-day."

For a second, as though he were part of the scenery, those violet eyes met his with a casual impersonal glance. Then their owner slowly spread out her own copy of the Mail.

"What's the news?" asked the statesman, drinking deep from his glass of water.

"Don't ask me," the girl answered, without looking up. "I've found something more entertaining than news. Do you know--the English papers run humorous columns! Only they aren't called that. They're called Personal Notices. And such notices!" She leaned across the table. "Listen to this: 'Dearest: Tender loving wishes to my dear one. Only to be with you now and always. None "fairer in my eyes."--'"

The man locked uncomfortably about him. "Hush!" he pleaded. "It doesn't sound very nice to me."

"Nice !" cried the girl. "Oh, but it is--quite nice. And so deliciously open and aboveboard. 'Your name is music to me. I love you more--'"

"What do we see to-day?" put in her father hastily.

"We're going down to the City and have a look at the Temple. Thackeray lived there once--and Oliver Goldsmith--"

"All right--the Temple it is."

"Then the Tower of London. It's full of the most romantic associations. Especially the Bloody Tower, where those poor little princes were murdered. Aren't you thrilled?"

"I am if you say so."

"You're a dear! I promise not to tell the people back in Texas that you showed any interest in kings and such--if you will show just a little. Otherwise I'll spread the awful news that you took off your hat when King George went by."

The statesman smiled. West felt that he, who had no business to, was smiling with him.

The waiter returned, bringing grapefruit, and the strawberries West had ordered. Without another look toward West, the girl put down her paper and began her breakfasting. As often as he dared, however, West looked at her. With patriotic pride he told himself: "Six months in Europe, and the most beautiful thing I've seen comes from back home!"

When he rose reluctantly twenty minutes later his two compatriots were still at table, discussing their plans for the day. As is usual in such cases, the girl arranged, the man agreed.

With one last glance in her direction, West went out on the parched pavement of Haymarket.

Slowly he walked back to his rooms. Work was waiting there for him; but instead of getting down to it, he sat on the balcony of his study, gazing out on the courtyard that had been his chief reason for selecting those apartments. Here, in the heart of the city, was a bit of the countryside transported--the green, trim, neatly tailored countryside that is the most satisfying thing in England. There were walls on which the ivy climbed high, narrow paths that ran between blooming beds of flowers, and opposite his windows a seldom-opened, most romantic gate. As he sat looking down he seemed to see there below him the girl of the Carlton. Now she sat on the rustic bench; now she bent above the envious flowers; now she stood at the gate that opened out to a hot sudden bit of the city.

And as he watched her there in the garden she would never enter, as he reflected unhappily that probably he would see her no more--the idea came to him.

At first he put it from him as absurd, impossible. She was, to apply a fine word much abused, a lady; he supposedly a gentleman. Their sort did not do such things. If he yielded to this temptation she would be shocked, angry, and from him would slip that one chance in a thousand he had--the chance of meeting her somewhere, some day.

And yet--and yet--She, too, had found the Agony Column entertaining and--quite nice. There was a twinkle in her eyes that bespoke a fondness for romance. She was human, fun-loving--and, above all, the joy of youth was in her heart.

Nonsense! West went inside and walked the floor. The idea was preposterous. Still--he smiled--it was filled with amusing possibilities. Too bad he must put it forever away and settle down to this stupid work!

Forever away? Well--

On the next morning, which was Saturday, West did not breakfast at the Carlton. The girl, however, did. As she and her father sat down the old man said: "I see you've got your Daily Mail."

"Of course!" she answered. "I couldn't do without it. Grapefruit --yes."

She began to read. Presently her cheeks flushed and she put the paper down.

"What is it?" asked the Texas statesman.

"To-day," she answered sternly, "you do the British Museum. You've put it off long enough."

The old man sighed. Fortunately he did not ask to see the Mail. If he had, a quarter way down the column of personal notices he would have been enraged--or perhaps only puzzled--to read:

CARLTON RESTAURANT: Nine A.M. Friday morning. Will the young woman who preferred grapefruit to strawberries permit the young man who had two plates of the latter to say he will not rest until he discovers some mutual friend, that they may meet and laugh over this column together?

Lucky for the young man who liked strawberries that his nerve had failed him and he was not present at the Carlton that morning! He would have been quite overcome to see the stern uncompromising look on the beautiful face of a lady at her grapefruit. So overcome, in fact, that he would probably have left the room at once, and thus not seen the mischievous smile that came in time to the lady's face --not seen that she soon picked up the paper again and read, with that smile, to the end of the column.

CHAPTER II

The next day was Sunday; hence it brought no Mail. Slowly it dragged along. At a ridiculously early hour Monday morning Geoffrey West was on the street, seeking his favorite newspaper. He found it, found the Agony Column--and nothing else. Tuesday morning again he rose early, still hopeful. Then and there hope died. The lady at the Canton deigned no reply.

Well, he had lost, he told himself. He had staked all on this one bold throw; no use. Probably if she thought of him at all it was to label him a cheap joker, a mountebank of the halfpenny press. Richly he deserved her scorn.

On Wednesday he slept late. He was in no haste to look into the Daily Mail; his disappointments of the previous days had been too keen. At last, while he was shaving, he summoned Walters, the caretaker of the building, and sent him out to procure a certain morning paper.

Walters came back bearing rich treasure, for in the Agony Column of that day West, his face white with lather, read joyously:

STRAWBERRY MAN: Only the grapefruit lady's kind heart and her great fondness for mystery and romance move her to answer. The strawberry-mad one may write one letter a day for seven days--to prove that he is an interesting person, worth knowing. Then--we shall see. Address: M. A. L., care Sadie Haight, Carlton Hotel.

All day West walked on air, but with the evening came the problem of those letters, on which depended, he felt, his entire future happiness. Returning from dinner, he sat down at his desk near the windows that looked out on his wonderful courtyard. The weather was still torrid, but with the night had come a breeze to fan the hot cheek of London. It gently stirred his curtains; rustled the papers on his desk.

He considered. Should he at once make known the eminently respectable person he was, the hopelessly respectable people he knew? Hardly! For then, on the instant, like a bubble bursting, would go for good all mystery and romance, and the lady of the grapefruit would lose all interest and listen to him no more. He spoke solemnly to his rustling curtains.

"No," he said. "We must have mystery and romance. But where--where shall we find them?"

On the floor above he heard the solid tramp of military boots belonging to his neighbor, Captain Stephen Fraser-Freer, of the Twelfth Cavalry, Indian Army, home on furlough from that colony beyond the seas. It was from that room overhead that romance and mystery were to come in mighty

store; but Geoffrey West little suspected it at the
moment. Hardly knowing what to say, but gaining
inspiration as he went along, he wrote the first of
seven letters to the lady at the Carlton. And the
epistle he dropped in the post box at midnight
follows here:

DEAR LADY OF THE GRAPEFRUIT: You are
very kind. Also, you are wise. Wise, because into
my clumsy little Personal you read nothing that was
not there. You knew it immediately for what it was-
-the timid tentative clutch of a shy man at the skirts
of Romance in passing. Believe me, old
Conservatism was with me when I wrote that
message. He was fighting hard. He followed me,
struggling, shrieking, protesting, to the post box
itself. But I whipped him. Glory be! I did for him.

We are young but once, I told him. After that, what
use to signal to Romance? The lady at least, I said,
will understand. He sneered at that. He shook his
silly gray head. I will admit he had me worried. But
now you have justified my faith in you. Thank you a
million times for that!

Three weeks I have been in this huge, ungainly,
indifferent city, longing for the States. Three weeks
the Agony Column has been my sole diversion. And
then--through the doorway of the Carlton
restaurant--you came--

It is of myself that I must write, I know. I will not,
then, tell you what is in my mind--the picture of you
I carry. It would mean little to you. Many Texan
gallants, no doubt, have told you the same while the

moon was bright above you and the breeze was softly whispering through the branches of--the branches of the--of the--

Confound it, I don't know! I have never been in Texas. It is a vice in me I hope soon to correct. All day I intended to look up Texas in the encyclopedia. But all day I have dwelt in the clouds. And there are no reference books in the clouds.

Now I am down to earth in my quiet study. Pens, ink and paper are before me. I must prove myself a person worth knowing.

From his rooms, they say, you can tell much about a man. But, alas! these peaceful rooms in Adelphi Terrace--I shall not tell the number--were sublet furnished. So if you could see me now you would be judging me by the possessions left behind by one Anthony Bartholomew. There is much dust on them. Judge neither Anthony nor me by that. Judge rather Walters, the caretaker, who lives in the basement with his gray-haired wife. Walters was a gardener once, and his whole life is wrapped up in the courtyard on which my balcony looks down. There he spends his time, while up above the dust gathers in the corners--

Does this picture distress you, my lady? You should see the courtyard! You would not blame Walters then. It is a sample of Paradise left at our door--that courtyard. As English as a hedge, as neat, as beautiful. London is a roar somewhere beyond; between our court and the great city is a magic gate, forever closed. It was the court that led me to take these rooms.

And, since you are one who loves mystery, I am going to relate to you the odd chain of circumstances that brought me here.

For the first link in that chain we must go back to Interlaken. Have you been there yet? A quiet little town, lying beautiful between two shimmering lakes, with the great Jungfrau itself for scenery. From the dining-room of one lucky hotel you may look up at dinner and watch the old-rose afterglow light the snow-capped mountain. You would not say then of strawberries: "I hate them." Or of anything else in all the world.

A month ago I was in Interlaken. One evening after dinner I strolled along the main street, where all the hotels and shops are drawn up at attention before the lovely mountain. In front of one of the shops I saw a collection of walking sticks and, since I needed one for climbing, I paused to look them over. I had been at this only a moment when a young Englishman stepped up and also began examining the sticks.

I had made a selection from the lot and was turning away to find the shopkeeper, when the Englishman spoke. He was lean, distinguished-looking, though quite young, and had that well-tubbed appearance which I am convinced is the great factor that has enabled the English to assert their authority over colonies like Egypt and India, where men are not so thoroughly bathed.

"Er--if you'll pardon me, old chap," he said. "Not that stick--if you don't mind my saying so. It's not tough enough for mountain work. I would suggest--"

To say that I was astonished is putting it mildly. If you know the English at all, you know it is not their habit to address strangers, even under the most pressing circumstances. Yet here was one of that haughty race actually interfering in my selection of a stick. I ended by buying the one he preferred, and he strolled along with me in the direction of my hotel, chatting meantime in a fashion far from British.

We stopped at the Kursaal, where we listened to the music, had a drink and threw away a few francs on the little horses. He came with me to the veranda of my hotel. I was surprised, when he took his leave, to find that he regarded me in the light of an old friend. He said he would call on me the next morning.

I made up my mind that Archibald Enwright--for that, he told me, was his name--was an adventurer down on his luck, who chose to forget his British exclusiveness under the stern necessity of getting money somehow, somewhere. The next day, I decided, I should be the victim of a touch.

But my prediction failed; Enwright seemed to have plenty of money. On that first evening I had mentioned to him that I expected shortly to be in London, and he often referred to the fact. As the time approached for me to leave Interlaken he began to throw out the suggestion that he should like to have me meet some of his people in England. This, also, was unheard of--against all precedent.

Nevertheless, when I said good-by to him he pressed into my hand a letter of introduction to his cousin, Captain Stephen Fraser-Freer, of the Twelfth Cavalry, Indian Army, who, he said, would be glad to make me at home in London, where he was on furlough at the time --or would be when I reached there.

"Stephen's a good sort," said Enwright. "He'll be jolly pleased to show you the ropes. Give him my best, old boy!"

Of course I took the letter. But I puzzled greatly over the affair. What could be the meaning of this sudden warm attachment that Archie had formed for me? Why should he want to pass me along to his cousin at a time when that gentleman, back home after two years in India, would be, no doubt, extremely busy? I made up my mind I would not present the letter, despite the fact that Archie had with great persistence wrung from me a promise to do so. I had met many English gentlemen, and I felt they were not the sort--despite the example of Archie--to take a wandering American to their bosoms when he came with a mere letter. By easy stages I came on to London. Here I met a friend, just sailing for home, who told me of some sad experiences he had had with letters of introduction-- of the cold, fishy, "My-dear-fellow-why-trouble-me-with-it?" stares that had greeted their presentation. Good-hearted men all, he said, but averse to strangers; an ever-present trait in the English--always excepting Archie.

So I put the letter to Captain Fraser-Freer out of my mind. I had business acquaintances here and a few English friends, and I found these, as always, courteous and charming. But it is to my advantage to meet as many people as may be, and after drifting about for a week I set out one afternoon to call on my captain. I told myself that here was an Englishman who had perhaps thawed a bit in the great oven of India. If not, no harm would be done.

It was then that I came for the first time to this house on Adelphi Terrace, for it was the address Archie had given me. Walters let me in, and I learned from him that Captain Fraser-Freer had not yet arrived from India. His rooms were ready--he had kept them during his absence, as seems to be the custom over here--and he was expected soon. Perhaps--said Walters--his wife remembered the date. He left me in the lower hail while he went to ask her.

Waiting, I strolled to the rear of the hall. And then, through an open window that let in the summer, I saw for the first time that courtyard which is my great love in London--the old ivy-covered walls of brick; the neat paths between the blooming beds; the rustic seat; the magic gate. It was incredible that just outside lay the world's biggest city, with all its poverty and wealth, its sorrows and joys, its roar and rattle. Here was a garden for Jane Austen to people with fine ladies and courtly gentlemen--here was a garden to dream in, to adore and to cherish.

When Walters came back to tell me that his wife was uncertain as to the exact date when the captain would return, I began to rave about that courtyard. At once he was my friend. I had been looking for quiet lodgings away from the hotel, and I was delighted to find that on the second floor, directly under the captain's rooms, there was a suite to be sublet.

Walters gave me the address of the agents; and, after submitting to an examination that could not have been more severe if I had asked for the hand of the senior partner's daughter, they let me come here to live. The garden was mine!

And the captain? Three days after I arrived I heard above me, for the first time, the tread of his military boots. Now again my courage began to fail. I should have preferred to leave Archie's letter lying in my desk and know my neighbor only by his tread above me. I felt that perhaps I had been presumptuous in coming to live in the same house with him. But I had represented myself to Walters as an acquaintance of the captain's and the caretaker had lost no time in telling me that "my friend" was safely home.

So one night, a week ago, I got up my nerve and went to the captain's rooms. I knocked. He called to me to enter and I stood in his study, facing him. He was a tall handsome man, fair-haired, mustached-- the very figure that you, my lady, in your boarding- school days, would have wished him to be. His manner, I am bound to admit, was not cordial.

"Captain," I began, "I am very sorry to intrude--" It wasn't the thing to say, of course, but I was fussed. "However, I happen to be a neighbor of yours, and I have here a letter of introduction from your cousin, Archibald Enwright. I met him in Interlaken and we became very good friends."

"Indeed!" said the captain.

He held out his hand for the letter, as though it were evidence at a court-martial. I passed it over, wishing I hadn't come. He read it through. It was a long letter, considering its nature. While I waited, standing by his desk--he hadn't asked me to sit down--I looked about the room. It was much like my own study, only I think a little dustier. Being on the third floor it was farther from the garden, consequently Walters reached there seldom.

The captain turned back and began to read the letter again. This was decidedly embarrassing. Glancing down, I happened to see on his desk an odd knife, which I fancy he had brought from India. The blade was of steel, dangerously sharp, the hilt of gold, carved to represent some heathen figure.

Then the captain looked up from Archie's letter and his cold gaze fell full upon me.

"My dear fellow," he said, "to the best of my knowledge, I have no cousin named Archibald Enwright."

A pleasant situation, you must admit! It's bad enough when you come to them with a letter from their mother, but here was I in this Englishman's rooms, boldly flaunting in his face a warm note of commendation from a cousin who did not exist!

"I owe you an apology," I said. I tried to be as haughty as he, and fell short by about two miles. "I brought the letter in good faith."

"No doubt of that," he answered.

"Evidently it was given me by some adventurer for purposes of his own," I went on; "though I am at a loss to guess what they could have been."

"I'm frightfully sorry--really," said he. But he said it with the London inflection, which plainly implies: "I'm nothing of the sort."

A painful pause. I felt that he ought to give me back the letter; but he made no move to do so. And, of course, I didn't ask for it.

"Ah--er--good night," said I and hurried toward the door.

"Good night," he answered, and I left him standing there with Archie's accursed letter in his hand.

That is the story of how I came to this house in Adelphi Terrace. There is mystery in it, you must admit, my lady. Once or twice since that uncomfortable call I have passed the captain on the stairs; but the halls are very dark, and for that I am grateful. I hear him often above me; in fact, I hear him as I write this.

Who was Archie? What was the idea? I wonder.

Ah, well, I have my garden, and for that I am indebted to Archie the garrulous. It is nearly midnight now. The roar of London has died away to a fretful murmur, and somehow across this baking town a breeze has found its way. It whispers over the green grass, in the ivy that climbs my wall, in the soft murky folds of my curtains. Whispers--what?

Whispers, perhaps, the dreams that go with this, the first of my letters to you. They are dreams that even I dare not whisper yet.

And so--good night.

THE STRAWBERRY MAN.

CHAPTER III

With a smile that betrayed unusual interest, the daughter of the Texas statesman read that letter on Thursday morning in her room at the Carlton. There was no question about it--the first epistle from the strawberry-mad one had caught and held her attention. All day, as she dragged her father through picture galleries, she found herself looking forward to another morning, wondering, eager.

But on the following morning Sadie Haight, the maid through whom this odd correspondence was passing, had no letter to deliver. The news rather disappointed the daughter of Texas. At noon she insisted on returning to the hotel for luncheon, though, as her father pointed out, they were far from the Canton at the time. Her journey was rewarded. Letter number two was waiting; and as she read she gasped.

DEAR LADY AT THE CARLTON: I am writing this at three in the morning, with London silent as the grave, beyond our garden. That I am so late in getting to it is not because I did not think of you all day yesterday; not because I did not sit down at my desk at seven last evening to address you. Believe me, only the most startling, the most appalling accident could have held me up.

That most startling, most appalling accident has happened.

I am tempted to give you the news at once in one striking and terrible sentence. And I could write that sentence. A tragedy, wrapped in mystery as impenetrable as a London fog, has befallen our quiet little house in Adelphi Terrace. In their basement room the Walters family, sleepless, overwhelmed, sit silent; on the dark stairs outside my door I hear at intervals the tramp of men on unhappy missions--But no; I must go back to the very start of it all:

Last night I had an early dinner at Simpson's, in the Strand--so early that I was practically alone in the restaurant. The letter I was about to write to you was uppermost in my mind and, having quickly dined, I hurried back to my rooms. I remember clearly that, as I stood in the street before our house fumbling for my keys, Big Ben on the Parliament Buildings struck the hour of seven. The chime of the great bell rang out in our peaceful thoroughfare like a loud and friendly greeting.

Gaining my study, I sat down at once to write. Over my head I could hear Captain Fraser-Freer moving about--attiring himself, probably, for dinner. I was thinking, with an amused smile, how horrified he would be if he knew that the crude American below him had dined at the impossible hour of six, when suddenly I heard, in that room above me, some stranger talking in a harsh determined tone. Then came the captain's answering voice, calmer, more dignified. This conversation went along for some time, growing each moment more excited. Though I could not distinguish a word of it, I had the uncomfortable feeling that there was a controversy on; and I remember feeling annoyed that any one should thus interfere with my composition of your letter, which I regarded as most important, you may be sure.

At the end of five minutes of argument there came the heavy thump-thump of men struggling above me. It recalled my college days, when we used to hear the fellows in the room above us throwing each other about in an excess of youth and high spirits. But this seemed more grim, more determined, and I did not like it.--However, I reflected that it was none of my business. I tried to think about my letter.

The struggle ended with a particularly heavy thud that shook our ancient house to its foundations. I sat listening, somehow very much depressed. There was no sound. It was not entirely dark outside--the long twilight--and the frugal Walters had not lighted the hall lamps. Somebody was coming down the stairs very quietly --but their creaking betrayed him. I waited for him to pass through the shaft of light that poured from the door open at my back. At that moment Fate intervened in the shape of a breeze through my windows, the door banged shut, and a heavy man rushed by me in the darkness and ran down the stairs. I knew he was heavy, because the passageway was narrow and he had to push me aside to get by. I heard him swear beneath his breath.

Quickly I went to a hall window at the far end that looked out on the street. But the front door did not open; no one came out. I was puzzled for a second then I reentered my room and hurried to my balcony. I could make out the dim figure of a man running through the garden at the rear--that garden of which I have so often spoken. He did not try to open the gate; he climbed it, and so disappeared from sight into the alley.

For a moment I considered. These were odd actions, surely; but was it my place to interfere? I remembered the cold stare in the eyes of Captain Fraser-Freer when I presented that letter. I saw him standing motionless in his murky study, as amiable as a statue. Would he welcome an intrusion from me now?

Finally I made up my mind to forget these things and went down to find Walters. He and his wife were eating their dinner in the basement. I told him what had happened. He said he had let no visitor in to see the captain, and was inclined to view my misgivings with a cold British eye. However, I persuaded him to go with me to the captain's rooms.

The captain's door was open. Remembering that in England the way of the intruder is hard, I ordered Walters to go first. He stepped into the room, where the gas flickered feebly in an aged chandelier.

"My God, sir!" said Walters, a servant even now.

And at last I write that sentence: Captain Fraser-Freer of the Indian Army lay dead on the floor, a smile that was almost a sneer on his handsome English face!

The horror of it is strong with me now as I sit in the silent morning in this room of mine which is so like the one in which the captain died. He had been stabbed just over the heart, and my first thought was of that odd Indian knife which I had seen lying on his study table. I turned quickly to seek it, but it was gone. And as I looked at the table it came to me that here in this dusty room there must be finger prints-- many finger prints.

The room was quite in order, despite those sounds of struggle. One or two odd matters met my eye. On the table stood a box from a florist in Bond Street. The lid had been removed and I saw that the box contained a number of white asters. Beside the box lay a scarf-pin--an emerald scarab. And not far from the captain's body lay what is known--owing to the German city where it is made--as a Homburg hat.

I recalled that it is most important at such times that nothing be disturbed, and I turned to old Walters. His face was like this paper on which I write; his knees trembled beneath him.

"Walters," said I, "we must leave things just as they are until the police arrive. Come with me while I notify Scotland Yard."

"Very good, sir," said Walters.

We went down then to the telephone in the lower hall, and I called up the Yard. I was told that an inspector would come at once and I went back to my room to wait for him.

You can well imagine the feelings that were mine as I waited. Before this mystery should be solved, I foresaw that I might be involved to a degree that was unpleasant if not dangerous. Walters would remember that I first came here as one acquainted with the captain. He had noted, I felt sure, the lack of intimacy between the captain and myself, once the former arrived from India. He would no doubt testify that I had been most anxious to obtain lodgings in the same house with Fraser-Freer. Then there was the matter of my letter from Archie. I must keep that secret, I felt sure. Lastly, there was not a living soul to back me up in my story of the quarrel that preceded the captain's death, of the man who escaped by way of the garden.

Alas, thought I, even the most stupid policeman can not fail to look upon me with the eye of suspicion!

In about twenty minutes three men arrived from Scotland Yard. By that time I had worked myself up into a state of absurd nervousness. I heard Walters let them in; heard them climb the stairs and walk about in the room overhead. In a short time Walters knocked at my door and told me that Chief Inspector Bray desired to speak to me. As I preceded the servant up the stairs I felt toward him as an accused murderer must feel toward the witness who has it in his power to swear his life away.

He was a big active man--Bray; blond as are so many Englishmen. His every move spoke efficiency. Trying to act as unconcerned as an innocent man should--but failing miserably, I fear--I related to him my story of the voices, the struggle, and the heavy man who had got by me in the hall and later climbed our gate. He listened without comment. At the end he said:

"You were acquainted with the captain?"

"Slightly," I told him. Archie's letter kept popping into my mind, frightening me. I had just met him-- that is all; through a friend of his--Archibald Enwright was the name."

"Is Enwright in London to vouch for you?"

"I'm afraid not. I last heard of him in Interlaken."

"Yes? How did you happen to take rooms in this house?"

"The first time I called to see the captain he had not yet arrived from India. I was looking for lodgings and I took a great fancy to the garden here."

It sounded silly, put like that. I wasn't surprised that the inspector eyed me with scorn. But I rather wished he hadn't.

Bray began to walk about the room, ignoring me.

"White asters; scarab pin; Homburg hat," he detailed, pausing before the table where those strange exhibits lay.

A constable came forward carrying newspapers in his hand.

"What is it?" Bray asked.

"The Daily Mail, sir," said the constable. "The issues of July twenty-seventh, twenty-eighth, twenty-ninth and thirtieth."

Bray took the papers in his hand, glanced at them and tossed them contemptuously into a wastebasket. He turned to Walters.

"Sorry, sir," said Walters; "but I was so taken aback! Nothing like this has ever happened to me before. I'll go at once--"

"No," replied Bray sharply. "Never mind. I'll attend to it--"

There was a knock at the door. Bray called "Come!" and a slender boy, frail but with a military bearing, entered.

"Hello, Walters!" he said, smiling. "What's up? I-"

He stopped suddenly as his eyes fell upon the divan where Fraser-Freer lay. In an instant he was at the dead man's side.

"Stephen!" he cried in anguish.

"Who are you?" demanded the inspector--rather rudely, I thought.

"It's the captain's brother, sir," put in Walters. "Lieutenant Norman Fraser-Freer, of the Royal Fusiliers."

There fell a silence.

"A great calamity, sir--" began Walters to the boy.

I have rarely seen any one so overcome as young Fraser-Freer. Watching him, it seemed to me that the affection existing between him and the man on the divan must have been a beautiful thing. He turned away from his brother at last, and Walters sought to give him some idea of what had happened.

"You will pardon me, gentlemen," said the lieutenant. "This has been a terrible shock! I didn't dream, of course--I just dropped in for a word with--with him. And now--"

We said nothing. We let him apologize, as a true Englishman must, for his public display of emotion.

"I'm sorry," Bray remarked in a moment, his eyes still shifting about the room--"especially as England may soon have great need of men like the captain. Now, gentlemen, I want to say this: I am the Chief of the Special Branch at the Yard. This is no ordinary murder. For reasons I can not disclose--and, I may add, for the best interests of the empire--news of the captain's tragic death must be kept for the present out of the newspapers. I mean, of course, the manner of his going. A mere death notice, you understand--the inference being that it was a natural taking off."

"I understand," said the lieutenant, as one who knows more than he tells.

"Thank you," said Bray. "I shall leave you to attend to the matter, as far as your family is concerned. You will take charge of the body. As for the rest of you, I forbid you to mention this matter outside."

And now Bray stood looking, with a puzzled air, at me.

"You are an American?" he said, and I judged he did not care for Americans.

"I am," I told him.

"Know any one at your consulate?" he demanded.

Thank heaven, I did! There is an under-secretary there named Watson--I went to college with him. I mentioned him to Bray.

"Very good," said the inspector. "You are free to go. But you must understand that you are an important witness in this case, and if you attempt to leave London you will be locked up."

So I came back to my rooms, horribly entangled in a mystery that is little to my liking. I have been sitting here in my study for some time, going over it again and again. There have been many footsteps on the stairs, many voices in the hall.

Waiting here for the dawn, I have come to be very sorry for the cold handsome captain. After all, he was a man; his very tread on the floor above, which it shall never hear again, told me that.

What does it all mean? Who was the man in the hall, the man who had argued so loudly, who had struck so surely with that queer Indian knife? Where is the knife now?

And, above all, what do the white asters signify? And the scarab scarf-pin? And that absurd Homburg hat?

Lady of the Canton, you wanted mystery. When I

wrote that first letter to you, little did I dream that I should soon have it to give you in overwhelming measure.

And--believe me when I say it--through all this your face has been constantly before me--your face as I saw it that bright morning in the hotel breakfast room. You have forgiven me, I know, for the manner in which I addressed you. I had seen your eyes and the temptation was great--very great.

It is dawn in the garden now and London is beginning to stir. So this time it is--good morning, my lady.

THE STRAWBERRY MAN.

CHAPTER IV

It is hardly necessary to intimate that this letter came as something of a shock to the young woman who received it. For the rest of that day the many sights of London held little interest for her--so little, indeed, that her perspiring father began to see visions of his beloved Texas; and once hopefully suggested an early return home. The coolness with which this idea was received plainly showed him that he was on the wrong track; so he sighed and sought solace at the bar.

That night the two from Texas attended His Majesty's Theater, where Bernard Shaw's latest play was being performed; and the witty Irishman would have been annoyed to see the scant attention one lovely young American in the audience gave his lines. The American in question retired at midnight, with eager thoughts turned toward the morning.

And she was not disappointed. When her maid, a stolid Englishwoman, appeared at her bedside early Saturday she carried a letter, which she handed over, with the turned-up nose of one who aids but does not approve. Quickly the girl tore it open.

DEAR Texas LADY: I am writing this late in the afternoon. The sun is casting long black shadows on the garden lawn, and the whole world is so bright and matter-of-fact I have to argue with myself to be convinced that the events of that tragic night through which I passed really happened.

The newspapers this morning helped to make it all seem a dream; not a line--not a word, that I can find. When I think of America, and how by this time the reporters would be swarming through our house if this thing had happened over there, I am the more astonished. But then, I know these English papers. The great Joe Chamberlain died the other night at ten, and it was noon the next day when the first paper to carry the story appeared--screaming loudly that it had scored a beat. It had. Other lands, other methods.

It was probably not difficult for Bray to keep journalists such as these in the dark. So their great ungainly sheets come out in total ignorance of a remarkable story in Adelphi Terrace. Famished for real news, they begin to hint at a huge war cloud on the horizon. Because tottering Austria has declared war on tiny Serbia, because the Kaiser is to-day hurrying, with his best dramatic effect, home to Berlin, they see all Europe shortly bathed in blood. A nightmare born of torrid days and tossing nights!

But it is of the affair in Adelphi Terrace that you no doubt want to hear. One sequel of the tragedy, which adds immeasurably to the mystery of it all, has occurred, and I alone am responsible for its discovery. But to go back:

I returned from mailing your letter at dawn this morning, very tired from the tension of the night. I went to bed, but could not sleep. More and more it was preying on my mind that I was in a most unhappy position. I had not liked the looks cast at me by Inspector Bray, or his voice when he asked how I came to live in this house. I told myself I should not be safe until the real murderer of the poor captain was found; and so I began to puzzle over the few clues in the case--especially over the asters, the scarab pin and the Homburg hat.

It was then I remembered the four copies of the Daily Mail that Bray had casually thrown into the waste-basket as of no interest. I had glanced over his shoulder as he examined these papers, and had seen that each of them was folded so that our favorite department --the Agony Column--was uppermost. It happened I had in my desk copies of the Mail for the past week. You will understand why.

I rose, found those papers, and began to read. It was then that I made the astounding discovery to which I have alluded.

For a time after making it I was dumb with amazement, so that no course of action came readily to mind. In the end I decided that the thing for me to do was to wait for Bray's return in the morning and then point out to him the error he had made in ignoring the Mail.

Bray came in about eight o'clock and a few minutes later I heard another man ascend the stairs. I was shaving at the time, but I quickly completed the operation and, slipping on a bathrobe, hurried up to the captain's rooms. The younger brother had seen to the removal of the unfortunate man's body in the night, and, aside from Bray and the stranger who had arrived almost simultaneously with him, there was no one but a sleepy-eyed constable there.

Bray's greeting was decidedly grouchy. The stranger, however--a tall bronzed man--made himself known to me in the most cordial manner. He told me he was Colonel Hughes, a close friend of the dead man; and that, unutterably shocked and grieved, he had come to inquire whether there was anything he might do. "Inspector," said I, "last night in this room you held in your hand four copies of the Daily Mail. You tossed them into that basket as of no account. May I suggest that you rescue those copies, as I have a rather startling matter to make clear to you?" Too grand an official to stoop to a waste-basket, he nodded to the constable. The latter brought the papers; and, selecting one from the lot,

I spread it out on the table. "The issue of July twenty-seventh," I said.

I pointed to an item half-way down the column of Personal Notices. You yourself, my lady, may read it there if you happen to have saved a copy. It ran as follows:

"RANGOON: The asters are in full bloom in the garden at Canterbury. They are very beautiful--especially the white ones."

Bray grunted, and opened his little eyes. I took up the issue of the following day--the twenty-eighth:

"RANGOON: We have been forced to sell father's stick-pin--the emerald scarab he brought home from Cairo."

I had Bray's interest now. He leaned heavily toward me, puffing. Greatly excited, I held before his eyes the issue of the twenty-ninth:

"RANGOON: Homburg hat gone forever--caught by a breeze--into the river."

"And finally," said I to the inspector, "the last message of all, in the issue of the thirtieth of July--on sale in the streets some twelve hours before Fraser-Freer was murdered. See!"

"RANGOON: To-night at ten. Regent Street. -- Y.O.G."

Bray was silent.

"I take it you are aware, Inspector," I said, "that for the past two years Captain Fraser-Freer was stationed at Rangoon."

Still he said nothing; just looked at me with those foxy little eyes that I was coming to detest. At last he spoke sharply:

"Just how," he demanded, "did you happen to discover those messages? You were not in this room last night after I left?" He turned angrily to the constable. "I gave orders--"

"No," I put in; "I was not in this room. I happened to have on file in my rooms copies of the Mail, and by the merest chance--"

I saw that I had blundered. Undoubtedly my discovery of those messages was too pat. Once again suspicion looked my way.

"Thank you very much," said Bray. "I'll keep this in mind."

"Have you communicated with my friend at the consulate?" I asked.

"Yes. That's all. Good morning."

So I went.

I had been back in my room some twenty minutes

when there came a knock on the door, and Colonel Hughes entered. He was a genial man, in the early forties I should say, tanned by some sun not English, and gray at the temples.

"My dear sir," he said without preamble, "this is a most appalling business!"

"Decidedly," I answered. "Will you sit down?"

"Thank you." He sat and gazed frankly into my eyes. "Policemen," he added meaningly, "are a most suspicious tribe--often without reason. I am sorry you happen to be involved in this affair, for I may say that I fancy you to be exactly what you seem. May I add that, if you should ever need a friend, I am at your service?"

I was touched; I thanked him as best I could. His tone was so sympathetic and before I realized it I was telling him the whole story--of Archie and his letter; of my falling in love with a garden; of the startling discovery that the captain had never heard of his cousin; and of my subsequent unpleasant position. He leaned back in his chair and closed his eyes.

"I suppose," he said, "that no man ever carries an unsealed letter of introduction without opening it to read just what praises have been lavished upon him. It is human nature--I have done it often. May I make so bold as to inquire--"

"Yes," said I. "It was unsealed and I did read it. Considering its purpose, it struck me as rather long.

There were many warm words for me--words beyond all reason in view of my brief acquaintance with Enwright. I also recall that he mentioned how long he had been in Interlaken, and that he said he expected to reach London about the first of August."

"The first of August," repeated the colonel. "That is to-morrow. Now--if you'll be so kind--just what happened last night?"

Again I ran over the events of that tragic evening--the quarrel; the heavy figure in the hall; the escape by way of the seldom-used gate.

"My boy," said Colonel Hughes as he rose to go, "the threads of this tragedy stretch far--some of them to India; some to a country I will not name. I may say frankly that I have other and greater interest in the matter than that of the captain's friend. For the present that is in strict confidence between us; the police are well-meaning, but they sometimes blunder. Did I understand you to say that you have copies of the Mail containing those odd messages?"

"Right here in my desk," said I. I got them for him.

"I think I shall take them--if I may," he said. "You will, of course, not mention this little visit of mine. We shall meet again. Good morning."

And he went away, carrying those papers with their strange signals to Rangoon.

Somehow I feel wonderfully cheered by his call. For the first time since seven last evening I begin to breathe freely again.

And so, lady who likes mystery, the matter stands on the afternoon of the last day of July, nineteen hundred and fourteen.

I shall mail you this letter to-night. It is my third to you, and it carries with it three times the dreams that went with the first; for they are dreams that live not only at night, when the moon is on the courtyard, but also in the bright light of day.

Yes--I am remarkably cheered. I realize that I have not eaten at all--save a cup of coffee from the trembling hand of Walters --since last night, at Simpson's. I am going now to dine. I shall begin with grapefruit. I realize that I am suddenly very fond of grapefruit.

How bromidic to note it--we have many tastes in common!

EX-STRAWBERRY MAN.

The third letter from her correspondent of the Agony Column increased in the mind of the lovely young woman at the Carlton the excitement and tension the second had created. For a long time, on the Saturday morning of its receipt, she sat in her room puzzling over the mystery of the house in Adelphi Terrace. When first she had heard that Captain Fraser-Freer, of the Indian Army, was dead of a knife wound over the heart, the news had shocked her like that of the loss of some old and dear friend. She had desired passionately the apprehension of his murderer, and had turned over and over in her mind the possibilities of white asters, a scarab pin and a Homburg hat.

Perhaps the girl longed for the arrest of the guilty man thus keenly because this jaunty young friend of hers--a friend whose name she did not know--to whom, indeed, she had never spoken--was so dangerously entangled in the affair. For from what she knew of Geoffrey West, from her casual glance in the restaurant and, far more, from his letters, she liked him extremely.

And now came his third letter, in which he related the connection of that hat, that pin and those asters with the column in the Mail which had first brought them together. As it happened, she, too, had copies of the paper for the first four days of the week. She went to her sitting-room, unearthed these copies, and--gasped! For from the column in Monday's paper stared up at her the cryptic words to Rangoon concerning asters in a garden at Canterbury. In the other three issues as well, she found the identical messages her strawberry man had quoted. She sat for a moment in deep thought; sat, in fact, until at her door came the enraged knocking of a hungry parent who had been waiting a full hour in the lobby below for her to join him at breakfast.

"Come, come!" boomed her father, entering at her invitation. "Don't sit here all day mooning. I'm hungry if you're not."

With quick apologies she made ready to accompany him down-stairs. Firmly, as she planned their campaign for the day, she resolved to put from her mind all thought of Adelphi Terrace. How well she succeeded may be judged from a speech made by her father that night just before dinner:

"Have you lost your tongue, Marian? You're as uncommunicative as a newly-elected office-holder. If you can't get a little more life into these expeditions of ours we'll pack up and head for home."

She smiled, patted his shoulder and promised to improve. But he appeared to be in a gloomy mood.

"I believe we ought to go, anyhow," he went on. "In my opinion this war is going to spread like a prairie fire. The Kaiser got back to Berlin yesterday. He'll sign the mobilization orders to-day as sure as fate. For the past week, on the Berlin Bourse, Canadian Pacific stock has been dropping. That means they expect England to come in."

He gazed darkly into the future. It may seem that, for an American statesman, he had an unusual grasp of European politics. This is easily explained by the fact that he had been talking with the bootblack at the Carlton Hotel.

"Yes," he said with sudden decision, "I'll go down to the steamship offices early Monday morning"

CHAPTER V

His daughter heard these words with a sinking heart. She had a most unhappy picture of herself boarding a ship and sailing out of Liverpool or Southampton, leaving the mystery that so engrossed her thoughts forever unsolved. Wisely she diverted her father's thoughts toward the question of food. She had heard, she said, that Simpson's, in the Strand, was an excellent place to dine. They would go there, and walk. She suggested a short detour that would carry them through Adelphi Terrace. It seemed she had always wanted to see Adelphi Terrace.

As they passed through that silent Street she sought to guess, from an inspection of the grim forbidding house fronts, back of which lay the lovely garden, the romantic mystery. But the houses were so very much like one another. Before one of them, she noted, a taxi waited.

After dinner her father pleaded for a music-hall as against what he called "some highfaluting, teacup English play." He won. Late that night, as they rode back to the Canton, special editions were being proclaimed in the streets. Germany was mobilizing!

The girl from Texas retired, wondering what epistolary surprise the morning would bring forth. It brought forth this:

DEAR DAUGHTER OF THE SENATE: Or is it Congress? I could not quite decide. But surely in one or the other of those August bodies your father sits when he is not at home in Texas or viewing Europe through his daughter's eyes. One look at him and I had gathered that.

But Washington is far from London, isn't it? And it is London that interests us most--though father's constituents must not know that. It is really a wonderful, an astounding city, once you have got the feel of the tourist out of your soul. I have been reading the most enthralling essays on it, written by a newspaper man who first fell desperately in love with it at seven--an age when the whole glittering town was symbolized for him by the fried-fish shop at the corner of the High Street. With him I have been going through its gray and furtive thoroughfares in the dead of night, and sometimes we have kicked an ash-barrel and sometimes a romance. Some day I might show that London to you--guarding you, of course, from the ash-barrels, if you are that kind. On second thoughts, you aren't. But I know that it is of Adelphi Terrace and a late captain in the Indian Army that you want to hear now. Yesterday, after my discovery of those messages in the Mail and the call of Captain Hughes, passed without incident. Last night I mailed you my third letter, and after wandering for a time amid the alternate glare and gloom of the city, I went back to my rooms and smoked on my balcony while about me the inmates of six million homes sweltered in the heat. Nothing happened. I felt a bit disappointed, a bit cheated, as one might feel on the first night spent at home after many successive visits to exciting plays. To-day, the first of August dawned, and still all was quiet. Indeed, it was not until this evening that further developments in the sudden death of Captain Fraser-Freer arrived to disturb me. These developments are strange ones surely, and I shall hasten to relate them.

I dined to-night at a little place in Soho. My waiter was Italian, and on him I amused myself with the Italian in Ten Lessons of which I am foolishly proud. We talked of Fiesole, where he had lived. Once I rode from Fiesole down the hill to Florence in the moonlight. I remember endless walls on which hung roses, fresh and blooming. I remember a gaunt nunnery and two-gray-robed sisters clanging shut the gates. I remember the searchlight from the military encampment, playing constantly over the Arno and the roofs--the eye of Mars that, here in Europe, never closes. And always the flowers nodding above me, stooping now and then to brush my face. I came to think that at the end Paradise, and not a second-rate hotel, was waiting. One may still take that ride, I fancy. Some day-- some day--

I dined in Soho. I came back to Adelphi Terrace in the hot, reeking August dusk, reflecting that the mystery in which I was involved was, after a fashion, standing still. In front of our house I noticed a taxi waiting. I thought nothing of it as I entered the murky hallway and climbed the familiar stairs.

My door stood open. It was dark in my study, save for the reflection of the lights of London outside. As I crossed the threshold there came to my nostrils the faint sweet perfume of lilacs. There are no lilacs in our garden, and if there were it is not the season. No, this perfume had been brought there by a woman--a woman who sat at my desk and raised her head as I entered.

"You will pardon this intrusion," she said in the correct careful English of one who has learned the speech from a book. "I have come for a brief word with you--then I shall go."

I could think of nothing to say. I stood gaping like a schoolboy.

"My word," the woman went on, "is in the nature of advice. We do not always like those who give us advice. None the less, I trust that you will listen."

I found my tongue then.

"I am listening," I said stupidly. "But first--a light--" And I moved toward the matches on the mantelpiece.

Quickly the woman rose and faced me. I saw then that she wore a veil--not a heavy veil, but a fluffy, attractive thing that was yet sufficient to screen her features from me.

"I beg of you," she cried, "no light!" And as I paused, undecided, she added, in a tone which suggested lips that pout: "It is such a little thing to ask--surely you will not refuse."

I suppose I should have insisted. But her voice was

charming, her manner perfect, and that odor of lilacs reminiscent of a garden I knew long ago, at home.

"Very well," said I.

"Oh--I am grateful to you," she answered. Her tone changed. "I understand that, shortly after seven o'clock last Thursday evening, you heard in the room above you the sounds of a struggle. Such has been your testimony to the police?"

"It has," said I.

"Are you quite certain as to the hour?" I felt that she was smiling at me. "Might it not have been later--or earlier?"

"I am sure it was just after seven," I replied. "I'll tell you why: I had just returned from dinner and while I was unlocking the door Big Ben on the House of Parliament struck--"

She raised her hand.

"No matter," she said, and there was a touch of iron in her voice. "You are no longer sure of that. Thinking it over, you have come to the conclusion that it may have been barely six-thirty when you heard the noise of a struggle."

"Indeed?" said I. I tried to sound sarcastic, but I was really too astonished by her tone.

"Yes--indeed!" she replied. "That is what you will tell Inspector Bray when next you see him. 'It may have been six-thirty,' you will tell him. 'I have thought it over and I am not certain.'"

"Even for a very charming lady," I said "I can not misrepresent the facts in a matter so important. It was after seven--"

"I am not asking you to do a favor for a lady," she replied. "I am asking you to do a favor for yourself. If you refuse the consequences may be most unpleasant."

"I'm rather at a loss--" I began.

She was silent for a moment. Then she turned and I felt her looking at me through the veil.

"Who was Archibald Enwright?" she demanded. My heart sank. I recognized the weapon in her hands. "The police," she went on, "do not yet know that the letter of introduction you brought to the captain was signed by a man who addressed Fraser-Freer as Dear Cousin, but who is completely unknown to the family. Once that information reaches Scotland Yard, your chance of escaping arrest is slim.

"They may not be able to fasten this crime upon you, but there will be complications most distasteful. One's liberty is well worth keeping--and then, too, before the case ends, there will be wide publicity--"

"'Well?" said I.

"That is why you are going to suffer a lapse of memory in the matter of the hour at which you heard that struggle. As you think it over, it is going to occur to you that it may have been six-thirty, not seven. Otherwise--"

"Go on."

"Otherwise the letter of introduction you gave to the captain will be sent anonymously to Inspector Bray."

"You have that letter!" I cried.

"Not I," she answered. "But it will be sent to Bray. It will be pointed out to him that you were posing under false colors. You could not escape!"

I was most uncomfortable. The net of suspicion seemed closing in about me. But I was resentful, too, of the confidence in this woman's voice.

"None the less," said I, "I refuse to change my testimony. The truth is the truth--"

The woman had moved to the door. She turned.

"To-morrow," she replied, "it is not unlikely you will see Inspector Bray. As I said, I came here to give you advice. You had better take it. What does it matter--a half-hour this way or that? And the difference is prison for you. Good night."

She was gone. I followed into the hall. Below, in the street, I heard the rattle of her taxi.

I went back into my room and sat down. I was upset, and no mistake. Outside my windows the continuous symphony of the city played on --the busses, the trains, the never-silent voices. I gazed out. What a tremendous acreage of dank brick houses and dank British souls! I felt horribly alone. I may add that I felt a bit frightened, as though that great city were slowly closing in on me.

Who was this woman of mystery? What place had she held in the life --and perhaps in the death--of Captain Fraser-Freer? Why should she come boldly to my rooms to make her impossible demand?

I resolved that, even at the risk of my own comfort, I would stick to the truth. And to that resolve I would have clung had I not shortly received another visit--this one far more inexplicable, far more surprising, than the first.

It was about nine o'clock when Walters tapped at my door and told me two gentlemen wished to see me. A moment later into my study walked Lieutenant Norman Fraser-Freer and a fine old gentleman with a face that suggested some faded portrait hanging on an aristocrat's wall. I had never seen him before.

"I hope it is quite convenient for you to see us," said young Fraser-Freer.

I assured him that it was. The boy's face was drawn

and haggard; there was terrible suffering in his eyes, yet about him hung, like a halo, the glory of a great resolution.

"May I present my father?" he said. "General Fraser-Freer, retired. We have come on a matter of supreme importance--"

The old man muttered something I could not catch. I could see that he had been hard hit by the loss of his elder son. I asked them to be seated; the general complied, but the boy walked the floor in a manner most distressing.

"I shall not be long," he remarked. "Nor at a time like this is one in the mood to be diplomatic. I will only say, sir, that we have come to ask of you a great--a very great favor indeed. You may not see fit to grant it. If that is the case we can not well reproach you. But if you can--"

"It is a great favor, sir!" broke in the general. "And I am in the odd position where I do not know whether you will serve me best by granting it or by refusing to do so."

"Father--please--if you don't mind--" The boy's voice was kindly but determined. He turned to me.

"Sir--you have testified to the police that it was a bit past seven when you heard in the room above the sounds of the struggle which--which--You understand."

In view of the mission of the caller who had

departed a scant hour previously, the boy's question startled me.

"Such was my testimony," I answered. "It was the truth."

"Naturally," said Lieutenant Fraser-Freer. "But--er--as a matter of fact, we are here to ask that you alter your testimony. Could you, as a favor to us who have suffered so cruel a loss--a favor we should never forget--could you not make the hour of that struggle half after six?"

I was quite overwhelmed.

"Your--reasons?" I managed at last to ask.

"I am not able to give them to you in full," the boy answered. "I can only say this: It happens that at seven o'clock last Thursday night I was dining with friends at the Savoy--friends who would not be likely to forget the occasion."

The old general leaped to his feet.

"Norman," he cried, "I can not let you do this thing! I simply will not--"

"Hush, father," said the boy wearily. "We have threshed it all out. You have promised--"

The old man sank back into the chair and buried his face in his hands.

"If you are willing to change your testimony," young Fraser-Freer went on to me, "I shall at once confess to the police that it was I who--who murdered my brother. They suspect me. They know that late last Thursday afternoon I purchased a revolver, for which, they believe, at the last moment I substituted the knife. They know that I was in debt to him; that we had quarreled about money matters; that by his death I, and I alone, could profit."

He broke off suddenly and came toward me, holding out his arms with a pleading gesture I can never forget.

"Do this for me!" he cried. "Let me confess! Let me end this whole horrible business here and now."

Surely no man had ever to answer such an appeal before.

"Why?" I found myself saying, and over and over I repeated it--"Why? Why?"

The lieutenant faced me, and I hope never again to see such a look in a man's eyes.

"I loved him!" he cried. "That is why. For his honor, for the honor of our family, I am making this request of you. Believe me, it is not easy. I can tell you no more than that. You knew my brother?"

"Slightly."

"Then, for his sake--do this thing I ask."

"But--murder--"

"You heard the sounds of a struggle. I shall say that we quarreled --that I struck in self-defense." He turned to his father. "It will mean only a few years in prison--I can bear that!" he cried. "For the honor of our name!"

The old man groaned, but did not raise his head. The boy walked back and forth over my faded carpet like a lion caged. I stood wondering what answer I should make.

"I know what you are thinking," said the lieutenant. "You can not credit your ears. But you have heard correctly. And now--as you might put it--it is up to you. I have been in your country." He smiled pitifully. "I think I know you Americans. You are not the sort to refuse a man when he is sore beset-- as I am."

I looked from him to the general and back again.

"I must think this over," I answered, my mind going at once to Colonel Hughes. "Later--say to-morrow-- you shall have my decision."

"To-morrow," said the boy, "we shall both be called before Inspector Bray. I shall know your answer then--and I hope with all my heart it will be yes."

There were a few mumbled words of farewell and he and the broken old man went out. As soon as the street door closed behind them I hurried to the telephone and called a number Colonel Hughes had given me. It was with a feeling of relief that I heard his voice come back over the wire. I told him I must see him at once. He replied that by a singular chance he had been on the point of starting for my rooms.

In the half-hour that elapsed before the coming of the colonel I walked about like a man in a trance. He was barely inside my door when I began pouring out to him the story of those two remarkable visits. He made little comment on the woman's call beyond asking me whether I could describe her; and he smiled when I mentioned lilac perfume. At mention of young Fraser-Freer's preposterous request he whistled.

"By gad!" he said. "Interesting--most interesting! I am not surprised, however. That boy has the stuff in him."

"But what shall I do?" I demanded.

Colonel Hughes smiled.

"It makes little difference what you do," he said. "Norman Fraser-Freer did not kill his brother, and that will be proved in due time." He considered for a moment. "Bray no doubt would be glad to have you alter your testimony, since he is trying to fasten the crime on the young lieutenant. On the whole, if I were you, I think that when the opportunity comes to-morrow I should humor the inspector.

"You mean--tell him I am no longer certain as to the hour of that struggle?"

"Precisely. I give you my word that young Fraser-Freer will not be permanently incriminated by such an act on your part. And incidentally you will be aiding me."

"Very well," said I. "But I don't understand this at all."

"No--of course not. I wish I could explain to you; but I can not. I will say this--the death of Captain Fraser-Freer is regarded as a most significant thing by the War Office. Thus it happens that two distinct hunts for his assassin are under way--one conducted by Bray, the other by me. Bray does not suspect that I am working on the case and I want to keep him in the dark as long as possible. You may choose which of these investigations you wish to be identified with."

"I think," said I, "that I prefer you to Bray."

"Good boy!" he answered. "You have not gone wrong. And you can do me a service this evening, which is why I was on the point of coming here, even before you telephoned me. I take it that you remember and could identify the chap who called himself Archibald Enwright --the man who gave you that letter to the captain?"

"I surely could," said I.

"Then, if you can spare me an hour, get your hat."

And so it happens, lady of the Carlton, that I have just been to Limehouse. You do not know where

Limehouse is and I trust you never will. It is picturesque; it is revolting; it is colorful and wicked. The weird odors of it still fill my nostrils; the sinister portrait of it is still before my eyes. It is the Chinatown of London --Limehouse. Down in the dregs of the town--with West India Dock Road for its spinal column--it lies, redolent of ways that are dark and tricks that are vain. Not only the heathen Chinee so peculiar shuffles through its dim-lit alleys, but the scum of the earth, of many colors and of many climes. The Arab and the Hindu, the Malayan and the Jap, black men from the Congo and fair men from Scandinavia --these you may meet there--the outpourings of all the ships that sail the Seven Seas. There many drunken beasts, with their pay in their pockets, seek each his favorite sin; and for those who love most the opium, there is, at all too regular intervals, the Sign of the Open Lamp.

We went there, Colonel Hughes and I. Up and down the narrow Causeway, yellow at intervals with the light from gloomy shops, dark mostly because of tightly closed shutters through which only thin jets found their way, we walked until we came and stood at last in shadow outside the black doorway of Harry San Li's so-called restaurant. We waited ten, fifteen minutes; then a man came down the Causeway and paused before that door. There was something familiar in his jaunty walk. Then the faint glow of the lamp that was the indication of Harry San's real business lit his pale face, and I knew that I had seen him last in the cool evening at Interlaken, where Limehouse could not have lived a moment, with the Jungfrau frowning down upon it.

"Enwright?" whispered Hughes.

"Not a doubt of it!" said I.

"Good!" he replied with fervor.

And now another man shuffled down the street and stood suddenly straight and waiting before the colonel.

"Stay with him," said Hughes softly. "Don't let him get out of your sight."

"Very good, sir," said the man; and, saluting, he passed on up the stairs and whistled softly at that black depressing door.

The clock above the Millwall Docks was striking eleven as the colonel and I caught a bus that should carry us back to a brighter, happier London. Hughes spoke but seldom on that ride; and, repeating his advice that I humor Inspector Bray on the morrow, he left me in the Strand.

So, my lady, here I sit in my study, waiting for that most important day that is shortly to dawn. A full evening, you must admit. A woman with the perfume of lilacs about her has threatened that unless I lie I shall encounter consequences most unpleasant. A handsome young lieutenant has begged me to tell that same lie for the honor of his family, and thus condemn him to certain arrest and imprisonment. And I have been down into hell, tonight and seen Archibald Enwright, of Interlaken, conniving with the devil.

I presume I should go to bed; but I know I can not
sleep. To-morrow is to be, beyond all question, a
red-letter day in the matter of the captain's murder.
And once again, against my will, I am down to play
a leading part.

The symphony of this great, gray, sad city is a mere
hum in the distance now, for it is nearly midnight. I
shall mail this letter to you--post it, I should say,
since I am in London--and then I shall wait in my
dim rooms for the dawn. And as I wait I shall be
thinking not always of the captain, or his brother, or
Hughes, or Limehouse and Enwright, but often--oh,
very often--of you.

In my last letter I scoffed at the idea of a great war.
But when we came back from Limehouse to-night
the papers told us that the Kaiser had signed the
order to mobilize. Austria in; Serbia in; Germany,
Russia and France in. Hughes tells me that England
is shortly to follow, and I suppose there is no doubt
of it. It is a frightful thing--this future that looms
before us; and I pray that for you at least it may
hold only happiness.

For, my lady, when I write good night, I speak it
aloud as I write; and there is in my voice more than
I dare tell you of now.

THE AGONY COLUMN MAN.

Not unwelcome to the violet eyes of the girl from
Texas were the last words of this letter, read in her
room that Sunday morning. But the lines predicting
England's early entrance into the war recalled to her

mind a most undesirable contingency. On the previous night, when the war extras came out confirming the forecast of his favorite bootblack, her usually calm father had shown signs of panic. He was not a man slow to act. And she knew that, putty though he was in her hands in matters which he did not regard as important, he could also be firm where he thought firmness necessary. America looked even better to him than usual, and he had made up his mind to go there immediately. There was no use in arguing with him.

At this point came a knock at her door and her father entered. One look at his face--red, perspiring and decidedly unhappy--served to cheer his daughter.

"Been down to the steamship offices," he panted, mopping his bald head. "They're open to-day, just like it was a week day--but they might as well be closed. There's nothing doing. Every boat's booked up to the rails; we can't get out of here for two weeks --maybe more."

"I'm sorry," said his daughter.

"No, you ain't! You're delighted! You think it's romantic to get caught like this. Wish I had the enthusiasm of youth." He fanned himself with a newspaper. "Lucky I went over to the express office yesterday and loaded up on gold. I reckon when the blow falls it'll be tolerable hard to cash checks in this man's town."

"That was a good idea."

"Ready for breakfast?" he inquired.

"Quite ready," she smiled.

They went below, she humming a song from a revue, while he glared at her. She was very glad they were to be in London a little longer. She felt she could not go, with that mystery still unsolved.

CHAPTER VI

The last peace Sunday London was to know in many weary months went by, a tense and anxious day. Early on Monday the fifth letter from the young man of the Agony Column arrived, and when the girl from Texas read it she knew that under no circumstances could she leave London now.

It ran:

DEAR LADY FROM HOME: I call you that because the word home has for me, this hot afternoon in London, about the sweetest sound word ever had. I can see, when I close my eyes, Broadway at midday; Fifth Avenue, gay and colorful, even with all the best people away; Washington Square, cool under the trees, lovely and desirable despite the presence everywhere of alien neighbors from the district to the South. I long for home with an ardent longing; never was London so cruel, so hopeless, so drab, in my eyes. For, as I write this, a constable sits at my elbow, and he and I are shortly to start for Scotland Yard. I have been arrested as a suspect in the case of Captain Fraser-Freer's murder!

I predicted last night that this was to be a red-letter day in the history of that case, and I also saw myself an unwilling actor in the drama. But little did I suspect the series of astonishing events that was to come with the morning; little did I dream that the net I have been dreading would to-day engulf me. I can scarcely blame Inspector Bray for holding me; what I can not understand is why Colonel Hughes--

But you want, of course, the whole story from the beginning; and I shall give it to you. At eleven o'clock this morning a constable called on me at my rooms and informed me that I was wanted at once by the Chief Inspector at the Yard.

We climbed--the constable and I--a narrow stone stairway somewhere at the back of New Scotland Yard, and so came to the inspector's room. Bray was waiting for us, smiling and confident. I remember --silly as the detail is--that he wore in his buttonhole a white rose. His manner of greeting me was more genial than usual. He began by informing me that the police had apprehended the man who, they believed, was guilty of the captain's murder.

"There is one detail to be cleared up," he said. "You told me the other night that it was shortly after seven o'clock when you heard the sounds of struggle in the room above you. You were somewhat excited at the time, and under similar circumstances men have been known to make mistakes. Have you considered the matter since? Is it not possible that you were in error in regard to the hour?"

I recalled Hughes' advice to humor the inspector; and I said that, having thought it over, I was not quite sure. It might have been earlier than seven-- say six-thirty.

"Exactly," said Bray. He seemed rather pleased. "The natural stress of the moment--I understand. Wilkinson bring in your prisoner. The constable addressed turned and left the room, coming back a moment later with Lieutenant Norman Fraser-Freer. The boy was pale; I could see at a glance that he had not slept for several nights.

"Lieutenant," said Bray very sharply, "will you tell me--is it true that your brother, the late captain, had loaned you a large sum of money a year or so ago?"

"Quite true," answered the lieutenant in a low voice.

"You and he had quarreled about the amount of money you spent?"

"Yes."

"By his death you became the sole heir of your father, the general. Your position with the money-lenders was quite altered. Am I right?"

"I fancy so."

"Last Thursday afternoon you went to the Army and Navy Stores and purchased a revolver. You already had your service weapon, but to shoot a man with a bullet from that would be to make the hunt of the police for the murderer absurdly simple."

The boy made no answer.

"Let us suppose," Bray went on, "that last Thursday evening at half after six you called on your brother in his rooms at Adelphi Terrace. There was an argument about money. You became enraged. You saw him and him alone between you and the fortune you needed so badly. Then --I am only supposing-- you noticed on his table an odd knife he had brought from India--safer--more silent--than a gun. You seized it--"

"Why suppose?" the boy broke in. "I'm not trying to conceal anything. You're right--I did it! I killed my brother! Now let us get the whole business over as soon as may be."

Into the face of Inspector Bray there came at that moment a look that has puzzling me ever since--a look that has recurred to my mind again and again,--in the stress and storm of this eventful day. It was only too evident that this confession came to him as a shock. I presume so easy a victory seemed hollow to him; he was wishing the boy had put up a fight. Policemen are probably like that.

"My boy," he said, "I am sorry for you. My course is clear. If you will go with one of my men--"

It was at this point that the door of the inspector's room opened and Colonel Hughes, cool and smiling, walked in. Bray chuckled at sight of the military man.

"Ah, colonel," he cried, "you make a good entrance! This morning, when I discovered that I had the honor of having you associated with me in the search for the captain's murderer, you were foolish enough to make a little wager--"

"I remember," Hughes answered. "A scarab pin against--a Homburg hat."

"Precisely," said Bray. "You wagered that you, and not I, would discover the guilty man. Well, Colonel, you owe me a scarab. Lieutenant Norman Fraser-Freer has just told me that he killed his brother, and I was on the point of taking down his full confession."

"Indeed!" replied Hughes calmly. "Interesting--most interesting! But before we consider the wager lost--before you force the lieutenant to confess in full--I should like the floor."

"Certainly," smiled Bray.

"When you were kind enough to let me have two of your men this morning," said Hughes, "I told you I contemplated the arrest of a lady. I have brought that lady to Scotland Yard with me." He stepped to the door, opened it and beckoned. A tall, blonde handsome woman of about thirty-five entered; and instantly to my nostrils came the pronounced odor of lilacs. "Allow me, Inspector," went on the colonel, "to introduce to you the Countess Sophie de Graf, late of Berlin, late of Delhi and Rangoon, now of 17 Leitrim Grove, Battersea Park Road."

The woman faced Bray; and there was a terrified, hunted look in her eyes.

"You are the inspector?" she asked.

"I am," said Bray.

"And a man--I can see that," she went on, her flashing angrily at Hughes. "I appeal to you to protect me from the brutal questioning of this--this fiend."

"You are hardly complimentary, Countess," Hughes smiled. "But I am willing to forgive you if you will tell the inspector the story that you have recently related to me."

The woman shut her lips tightly and for a long moment gazed into the eyes of Inspector Bray.

"He"--she said at last, nodding in the direction of Colonel Hughes --"he got it out of me--how, I don't know."

"Got what out of you?" Bray's little eyes were blinking.

"At six-thirty o'clock last Thursday evening," said the woman, "I went to the rooms of Captain Fraser-

Freer, in Adelphi Terrace. An argument arose. I seized from his table an Indian dagger that was lying there--I stabbed him just above the heart!"

In that room in Scotland Yard a tense silence fell. For the first time we were all conscious of a tiny clock on the inspector's desk, for it ticked now with a loudness sudden and startling. I gazed at the faces about me. Bray's showed a momentary surprise--then the mask fell again. Lieutenant Fraser-Freer was plainly amazed. On the face of Colonel Hughes I saw what struck me as an open sneer.

"Go on, Countess," he smiled.

She shrugged her shoulders and turned toward him a disdainful back. Her eyes were all for Bray.

"It's very brief, the story," she said hastily--I thought almost apologetically. "I had known the captain in Rangoon. My husband was in business there--an exporter of rice--and Captain Fraser-Freer came often to our house. We--he was a charming man, the captain--"Go on!" ordered Hughes.

"We fell desperately in love," said the countess. "When he returned to England, though supposedly on a furlough, he told me he would never return to Rangoon. He expected a transfer to Egypt. So it was arranged that I should desert my husband and follow on the next boat. I did so--believing in the captain--thinking he really cared for me--I gave up everything for him. And then--"

Her voice broke and she took out a handkerchief.

Again that odor of lilacs in the room.

"For a time I saw the captain often in London; and then I began to notice a change. Back among his own kind, with the lonely days in India a mere memory--he seemed no longer to--to care for me. Then--last Thursday morning--he called on me to tell me that he was through; that he would never see me again--in fact, that he was to marry a girl of his own people who had been waiting--"

The woman looked piteously about at us.

"I was desperate," she pleaded. "I had given up all that life held for me--given it up for a man who now looked at me coldly and spoke of marrying another. Can you wonder that I went in the evening to his rooms--went to plead with him--to beg, almost on my knees? It was no use. He was done with me--he said that over and over. Overwhelmed with blind rage and despair, I snatched up that knife from the table and plunged it into his heart. At once I was filled with remorse. I--"

"One moment," broke in Hughes. "You may keep the details of your subsequent actions until later. I should like to compliment you, Countess. You tell it better each time."

He came over and faced Bray. I thought there was a distinct note of hostility in his voice.

"Checkmate, Inspector!" he said. Bray made no reply. He sat there staring up at the colonel, his face turned to stone.

"The scarab pin," went on Hughes, "is not yet forthcoming. We are tied for honors, my friend. You have your confession, but I have one to match it."

"All this is beyond me," snapped Bray.

"A bit beyond me, too," the colonel answered. "Here are two people who wish us to believe that on the evening of Thursday last, at half after six of the clock, each sought out Captain Fraser-Freer in his rooms and murdered him."

He walked to the window and then wheeled dramatically.

"The strangest part of it all is," he added, "that at six-thirty o'clock last Thursday evening, at an obscure restaurant in Soho --Frigacci's--these two people were having tea together !"

I must admit that, as the colonel calmly offered this information, I suddenly went limp all over at a realization of the endless maze of mystery in which we were involved. The woman gave a little cry and Lieutenant Fraser-Freer leaped to his feet.

"How the devil do you know that?" he cried.

"I know it," said Colonel Hughes, "because one of my men happened to be having tea at a table near by. He happened to be having tea there for the reason that ever since the arrival of this lady in London, at the request of--er--friends in India, I have been keeping track of her every move; just as I kept watch over your late brother, the captain."

Without a word Lieutenant Fraser-Freer dropped into a chair and buried his face in his hands.

"I'm sorry, my son," said Hughes. "Really, I am. You made a heroic effort to keep the facts from coming out--a man's-size effort it was. But the War Office knew long before you did that your brother had succumbed to this woman's lure--that he was serving her and Berlin, and not his own country, England."

Fraser-Freer raised his head. When he spoke there was in his voice an emotion vastly more sincere than that which had moved him when he made his absurd confession.

"The game's up," he said. "I have done all I could. This will kill my father, I am afraid. Ours has been an honorable name, Colonel; you know that--a long line of military men whose loyalty to their country has never before been in question. I thought my confession would end the whole nasty business, that the investigations would stop, and that I might be able to keep forever unknown this horrible thing about him--about my brother."

Colonel Hughes laid his hand on the boy's shoulder, and the latter went on: "They reached me--those frightful insinuations about Stephen--in a round about way; and when he came home from India I resolved to watch him. I saw him go often to the house of this woman. I satisfied myself that she was the same one involved in the stories coming from

Rangoon; then, under another name, I managed to meet her. I hinted to her that I myself was none too loyal; not completely, but to a limited extent, I won her confidence. Gradually I became convinced that my brother was indeed disloyal to his country, to his name, to us all. It was at that tea time you have mentioned when I finally made up my mind. I had already bought a revolver; and, with it in my pocket, I went to the Savoy for dinner."

He rose and paced the floor.

"I left the Savoy early and went to Stephen's rooms. I was resolved to have it out with him, to put the matter to him bluntly; and if he had no explanation to give me I intended to kill him then and there. So, you see, I was guilty in intention if not in reality. I entered his study. It was filled with strangers. On his sofa I saw my brother Stephen lying--stabbed above the heart--dead!" There was a moment's silence. "That is all," said Lieutenant Fraser-Freer.

"I take it," said Hughes kindly, "that we have finished with the lieutenant. Eh, Inspector?"

"Yes," said Bray shortly. "You may go."

"Thank you," the boy answered. As he went out he said brokenly to Hughes: "I must find him--my father."

Bray sat in his chair, staring hard ahead, his jaw thrust out angrily. Suddenly he turned on Hughes.

"You don't play fair," he said. "I wasn't told

anything of the status of the captain at the War Office. This is all news to me."

"Very well," smiled Hughes. "The bet is off if you like."

"No, by heaven!" Bray cried. "It's still on, and I'll win it yet. A fine morning's work I suppose you think you've done. But are we any nearer to finding the murderer? Tell me that."

"Only a bit nearer, at any rate," replied Hughes suavely. "This lady, of course, remains in custody."

"Yes, yes," answered the inspector. "Take her away!" he ordered.

A constable came forward for the countess and Colonel Hughes gallantly held open the door.

"You will have an opportunity, Sophie," he said, "to think up another story. You are clever--it will not he hard."

She gave him a black look and went out. Bray got up from his desk. He and Colonel Hughes stood facing each other across a table, and to me there was something in the manner of each that suggested eternal conflict.

"Well?" sneered Bray.

"There is one possibility we have overlooked," Hughes answered. He turned toward me and I was startled by the coldness in his eyes. "Do you know, Inspector," he went on, "that this American came to London with a letter of introduction to the captain--a letter from the captain's cousin, one Archibald Enwright? And do you know that Fraser-Freer had no cousin of that name?"

"No!" said Bray.

"It happens to be the truth," said Hughes. "The American has confessed as much to me."

"Then," said Bray to me, and his little blinking eyes were on me with a narrow calculating glance that sent the shivers up and down my spine, "you are under arrest. I have exempted you so far because of your friend at the United States Consulate. That exemption ends now."

I was thunderstruck. I turned to the colonel, the man who had suggested that I seek him out if I needed a friend--the man I had looked to to save me from just such a contingency as this. But his eyes were quite fishy and unsympathetic.

"Quite correct, Inspector," he said. "Lock him up!" And as I began to protest he passed very close to me and spoke in a low voice: "Say nothing. Wait!"

I pleaded to be allowed to go back to my rooms, to communicate with my friends, and pay a visit to our consulate and to the Embassy; and at the colonel's suggestion Bray agreed to this somewhat irregular course. So this afternoon I have been abroad with a constable, and while I wrote this long letter to you he has been fidgeting in my easy chair. Now he informs me that his patience is exhausted and that I must go at once. So there is no time to wonder; no time to speculate as to the future, as to the colonel's sudden turn against me or the promise of his whisper in my ear. I shall, no doubt, spend the night behind those hideous, forbidding walls that your guide has pointed out to you as New Scotland Yard. And when I shall write again, when I shall end this series of letters so filled with--

The constable will not wait. He is as impatient as a child. Surely he is lying when he says I have kept him here an hour.

Wherever I am, dear lady, whatever be the end of this amazing tangle, you may be sure the thought of you--Confound the man!

YOURS, IN DURANCE VILE.

This fifth letter from the young man of the Agony Column arrived at the Carlton Hotel, as the reader may recall, on Monday morning, August the third. And it represented to the girl from Texas the climax of the excitement she had experienced in the matter of the murder in Adelphi Terrace. The news that her pleasant young friend--whom she did not know-- had been arrested as a suspect in the case, inevitable as it had seemed for days, came none the less as an unhappy shock. She wondered whether there was anything she could do to help. She even considered going to Scotland Yard and, on the ground that her father was a Congressman from Texas, demanding the immediate release of her strawberry man.

Sensibly, however, she decided that Congressmen from Texas meant little in the life of the London police. Besides, she night have difficulty in explaining to that same Congressman how she happened to know all about a crime that was as yet unmentioned in the newspapers.

So she reread the latter portion of the fifth letter, which pictured her hero marched off ingloriously to Scotland Yard and with a worried little sigh, went below to join her father.

CHAPTER VII

In the course of the morning she made several mysterious inquiries of her parent regarding nice points of international law as it concerned murder, and it is probable that he would have been struck by the odd nature of these questions had he not been unduly excited about another matter.

"I tell you, we've got to get home!" he announced gloomily. "The German troops are ready at Aix-la-Chapelle for an assault on Liege. Yes, sir--they're going to strike through Belgium! Know what that means? England in the war! Labor troubles; suffragette troubles; civil war in Ireland--these things will melt winter in Texas. They'll go in. It would be national suicide if they didn't."

His daughter stared at him. She was unaware that it was the bootblack at the Canton he was now quoting. She began to think he knew more about foreign affairs than she had given him credit for.

"Yes, sir," he went on; "we've got to travel--fast. This won't be a healthy neighborhood for non-combatants when the ruction starts. I'm going if I have to buy a liner!"

"Nonsense!" said the girl. "This is the chance of a lifetime. I won't be cheated out of it by a silly old dad. Why, here we are, face to face with history!"

"American history is good enough for me," he spread-eagled. "What are you looking at?"

"Provincial to the death!" she said thoughtfully. "You old dear --I love you so! Some of our statesmen over home are going to look pretty foolish now in the face of things they can't understand I hope you're not going to be one of them."

"Twaddle!" he cried. "I'm going to the steamship offices to-day and argue as I never argued for a vote."

His daughter saw that he was determined; and, wise from long experience, she did not try to dissuade him.

London that hot Monday was a city on the alert, a city of hearts heavy with dread. The rumors in one special edition of the papers were denied in the next and reaffirmed in the next. Men who could look into the future walked the streets with faces far from happy. Unrest ruled the town. And it found its echo in the heart of the girl from Texas as she thought of her young friend of the Agony Column "in durance vile" behind the frowning walls of Scotland Yard.

That afternoon her father appeared, with the beaming mien of the victor, and announced that for a stupendous sum he had bought the tickets of a man who was to have sailed on the steamship Saronia three days hence.

"The boat train leaves at ten Thursday morning," he said. "Take your last look at Europe and be ready."

Three days! His daughter listened with sinking heart. Could she in three days' time learn the end of that strange mystery, know the final fate of the man who had first addressed her so unconventionally in a public print? Why, at the end of three days he might still be in Scotland Yard, a prisoner! She could not leave if that were true--she simply could not. Almost she was on the point of telling her father the story of the whole affair, confident that she could soothe his anger and enlist his aid. She decided to wait until the next morning; and, if no letter came then--

But on Tuesday morning a letter did come and the beginning of it brought pleasant news. The beginning--yes. But the end! This was the letter:

DEAR ANXIOUS LADY: Is it too much for me to assume that you have been just that, knowing as you did that I was locked up for the murder of a captain in the Indian Army, with the evidence all against me and hope a very still small voice indeed?

Well, dear lady, be anxious no longer. I have just lived through the most astounding day of all the astounding days that have been my portion since last Thursday. And now, in the dusk, I sit again in my rooms, a free man, and write to you in what peace and quiet I can command after the startling adventure through which I have recently passed.

Suspicion no longer points to me; constables no longer eye me; Scotland Yard is not even slightly interested in me. For the murderer of Captain Fraser-Freer has been caught at last!

Sunday night I spent ingloriously in a cell in Scotland Yard. I could not sleep. I had so much to think of--you, for example, and at intervals how I might escape from the folds of the net that had closed so tightly about me. My friend at the consulate, Watson, called on me late in the evening; and he was very kind. But there was a note lacking in his voice, and after, he was gone the terrible certainty came into my mind--he believed that I was guilty after all.

The night passed, and a goodly portion of to-day went by--as the poets say--with lagging feet. I thought of London, yellow in the sun. I thought of the Carlton--I suppose there are no more strawberries by this time. And my waiter--that stiff-backed Prussian--is home in Deutschland now, I presume, marching with his regiment. I thought of you.

At three o'clock this afternoon they came for me and I was led back to the room belonging to Inspector Bray. When I entered, however, the inspector was not there--only Colonel Hughes, immaculate and self-possessed, as usual, gazing out the window into the cheerless stone court. He turned when I entered. I suppose I must have had a most woebegone appearance, for a look of regret crossed his face.

"My dear fellow," he cried, "my most humble apologies! I intended to have you released last night. But, believe me, I have been frightfully busy."

I said nothing. What could I say? The fact that he had been busy struck me as an extremely silly excuse. But the inference that my escape from the toils of the law was imminent set my heart to thumping.

"I fear you can never forgive me for throwing you over as I did yesterday," he went on. "I can only say that it was absolutely necessary--as you shall shortly understand."

I thawed a bit. After all, there was an unmistakable sincerity in his voice and manner.

"We are waiting for Inspector Bray," continued the colonel. "I take it you wish to see this thing through?"

"To the end," I answered.

"Naturally. The inspector was called away yesterday immediately after our interview with him. He had business on the Continent, I understand. But fortunately I managed to reach him at Dover and he has come back to London. I wanted him, you see, because I have found the murderer of Captain Fraser-Freer."

I thrilled to hear that, for from my point of view it was certainly a consummation devoutly to be wished. The colonel did not speak again. In a few minutes the door opened and Bray came in. His clothes looked as though he had slept in them; his little eyes were bloodshot. But in those eyes there was a fire I shall never forget. Hughes bowed.

"Good afternoon, Inspector," he said. "I'm really sorry I had to interrupt you as I did; but I most awfully wanted you to know that you owe me a Homburg hat." He went closer to the detective. "You see, I have won that wager. I have found the man who murdered Captain Fraser-Freer."

Curiously enough, Bray said nothing. He sat down at his desk and idly glanced through the pile of mail that lay upon it. Finally he looked up and said in a weary tone:

"You're very clever, I'm sure, Colonel Hughes."

"Oh--I wouldn't say that," replied Hughes. "Luck was with me --from the first. I am really very glad to have been of service in the matter, for I am convinced that if I had not taken part in the search it would have gone hard with some innocent man."

Bray's big pudgy hands still played idly with the mail on his desk. Hughes went on: "Perhaps, as a clever detective, you will be interested in the series of events which enabled me to win that Homburg hat? You have heard, no doubt, that the man I have caught is Von der Herts--ten years ago the best secret-service man in the employ of the Berlin government, but for the past few years mysteriously missing from our line of vision. We've been wondering about him--at the War Office."

The colonel dropped into a chair, facing Bray.

"You know Von der Herts, of course?" he remarked casually.

"Of course," said Bray, still in that dead tired voice.

"He is the head of that crowd in England," went on Hughes. "Rather a feather in my cap to get him--but I mustn't boast. Poor Fraser-Freer would have got him if I hadn't--only Von der Herts had the luck to get the captain first."

Bray raised his eyes.

"You said you were going to tell me--" he began.

"And so I am," said Hughes. "Captain Fraser-Freer got in rather a mess in India and failed of promotion. It was suspected that he was discontented, soured on the Service; and the Countess Sophie de Graf was set to beguile him with her charms, to kill his loyalty and win him over to her crowd.

"It was thought she had succeeded--the Wilhelmstrasse thought so--we at the War Office thought so, as long as he stayed in India.

"But when the captain and the woman came on to London we discovered that we had done him a great injustice. He let us know, when the first chance offered, that he was trying to redeem himself, to round up a dangerous band of spies by pretending to be one of them. He said that it was his mission in London to meet Von der Herts, the greatest of them all; and that, once he had located this man, we would hear from him again. In the weeks that followed I continued to keep a watch on the countess; and I kept track of the captain, too, in a general way, for I'm ashamed to say I was not quite sure of him."

The colonel got up and walked to the window; then turned and continued: "Captain Fraser-Freer and Von der Herts were completely unknown to each other. The mails were barred as a means of communication; but Fraser-Freer knew that in some way word from the master would reach him, and he had had a tip to watch the personal column of the Daily Mail. Now we have the explanation of those four odd messages. From that column the man from Rangoon learned that he was to wear a white aster in his button-hole, a scarab pin in his tie, a Homburg hat on his head, and meet Von der Herts at Ye Old Gambrinus Restaurant in Regent Street, last Thursday night at ten o'clock. As we know, he made all arrangements to comply with those directions. He made other arrangements as well. Since it was out of the question for him to come to

Scotland Yard, by skillful maneuvering he managed to interview an inspector of police at the Hotel Cecil. It was agreed that on Thursday night Von der Herts would be placed under arrest the moment he made himself known to the captain."

Hughes paused. Bray still idled with his pile of letters, while the colonel regarded him gravely.

"Poor Fraser-Freer!" Hughes went on. "Unfortunately for him, Von der Herts knew almost as soon as did the inspector that a plan was afoot to trap him. There was but one course open to him: He located the captain's lodgings, went there at seven that night, and killed a loyal and brave Englishman where he stood."

A tense silence filled the room. I sat on the edge of my chair, wondering just where all this unwinding of the tangle was leading us.

"I had little, indeed, to work on," went on Hughes. "But I had this advantage: the spy thought the police, and the police alone, were seeking the murderer. He was at no pains to throw me off his track, because he did not suspect that I was on it. For weeks my men had been watching the countess. I had them continue to do so. I figured that sooner or later Von der Herts would get in touch with her. I was right. And when at last I saw with my own eyes the man who must, beyond all question, be Von der Herts, I was astounded, my dear Inspector, I was overwhelmed."

"Yes?" said Bray.

"I set to work then in earnest to connect him with that night in Adelphi Terrace. All the finger marks in the captain's study were for some reason destroyed, but I found others outside, in the dust on that seldom-used gate which leads from the garden. Without his knowing, I secured from the man I suspected the imprint of his right thumb. A comparison was startling. Next I went down into Fleet Street and luckily managed to get hold of the typewritten copy sent to the Mail bearing those four messages. I noticed that in these the letter a was out of alignment. I maneuvered to get a letter written on a typewriter belonging to my man. The a was out of alignment. Then Archibald Enwright, a renegade and waster well known to us as serving other countries, came to England. My man and he met--at Ye Old Gambrinus, in Regent Street. And finally, on a visit to the lodgings of this man who, I was now certain, was Von der Herts, under the mattress of his bed I found this knife."

And Colonel Hughes threw down upon the inspector's desk the knife from India that I had last seen in the study of Captain Fraser-Freer.

"All these points of evidence were in my hands yesterday morning in this room," Hughes went on. "Still, the answer they gave me was so unbelievable, so astounding, I was not satisfied; I wanted even stronger proof. That is why I directed suspicion to my American friend here. I was waiting. I knew that at last Von der Herts realized the danger he was in. I felt that if opportunity were offered he would attempt to escape from England; and then our proofs of his guilt would be unanswerable, despite his cleverness. True enough, in the afternoon he secured the release of the countess, and together they started for the Continent. I was lucky enough to get him at Dover-- and glad to let the lady go on."

And now, for the first time, the startling truth struck me full in the face as Hughes smiled down at his victim.

"Inspector Bray," he said, "or Von der Herts, as you choose, I arrest you on two counts: First, as the head of the Wilhelmstrasse spy system in England; second, as the murderer of Captain Fraser-Freer. And, if you will allow me, I wish to compliment you on your efficiency."

Bray did not reply for a moment. I sat numb in my chair. Finally the inspector looked up. He actually tried to smile.

"You win the hat," he said, "but you must go to Homburg for it. I will gladly pay all expenses."

"Thank you," answered Hughes. "I hope to visit your country before long; but I shall not be occupied with hats. Again I congratulate you. You were a bit careless, but your position justified that. As head of the department at Scotland Yard given over to the hunt for spies, precaution doubtless struck you as unnecessary. How unlucky for poor Fraser-Freer that it was to you he went to arrange or your own arrest! I got that information from a clerk at the Cecil. You were quite right, from your point of view, to kill him. And, as I say, you could afford to be rather reckless. You had arranged that when the news of his murder came to Scotland Yard you yourself would be on hand to conduct the search for the guilty man. A happy situation, was it not?"

"It seemed so at the time," admitted Bray; and at last I thought I detected a note of bitterness in his voice.

"I'm very sorry--really," said Hughes. "To-day, or to-morrow at the latest, England will enter the war. You know what that means, Von der Herts. The Tower of London--and a firing squad!"

Deliberately he walked away from the inspector, and stood facing the window. Von der Herts was fingering idly that Indian knife which lay on his desk. With a quick hunted look about the room, he raised his hand; and before I could leap forward to stop him he had plunged the knife into his heart.

Colonel Hughes turned round at my cry, but even at what met his eyes now that Englishman was imperturbable.

"Too bad!" he said. "Really too bad! The man had courage and, beyond all doubt, brains. But--this is most considerate of him. He has saved me such a lot of trouble."

The colonel effected my release at once; and he and I walked down Whitehall together in the bright sun that seemed so good to me after the bleak walls of the Yard. Again he apologized for turning suspicion my way the previous day; but I assured him I held no grudge for that.

"One or two things I do not understand," I said. "That letter I brought from Interlaken--"

"Simple enough," he replied. "Enwright--who, by the way, is now in the Tower--wanted to communicate with Fraser-Freer, who he supposed was a loyal member of the band. Letters sent by post seemed dangerous. With your kind assistance he informed the captain of his whereabouts and the date of his imminent arrival in London. Fraser-Freer, not wanting you entangled in his plans, eliminated you by denying the existence of this cousin--the truth, of course."

"Why," I asked, "did the countess call on me to demand that I alter my testimony?"

"Bray sent her. He had rifled Fraser-Freer's desk and he held that letter from Enwright. He was most anxious to fix the guilt upon the young lieutenant's head. You and your testimony as to the hour of the crime stood in the way. He sought to intimidate you with threats--"

"But--"

"I know--you are wondering why the countess confessed to me next day. I had the woman in rather a funk. In the meshes of my rapid-fire questioning she became hopelessly involved. This was because she was suddenly terrified she realized I must have been watching her for weeks, and that perhaps Von der Herts was not so immune from suspicion as he supposed. At the proper moment I suggested that I might have to take her to Inspector Bray. This gave her an idea. She made her fake confession to reach his side; once there, she warned him of his danger and they fled together."

We walked along a moment in silence. All about us the lurid special editions of the afternoon were flaunting their predictions of the horror to come. The face of the colonel was grave.

"How long had Von der Herts held his position at the Yard?" I asked.

"For nearly five years," Hughes answered.

"It seems incredible," I murmured.

"So it does," he answered; "but it is only the first of many incredible things that this war will reveal. Two months from now we shall all have forgotten it in the face of new revelations far more unbelievable." He sighed. "If these men about us realized the terrible ordeal that lies ahead! Misgoverned; unprepared--I shudder at the thought of the sacrifices we must make, many of them in vain. But I suppose that somehow, some day, we shall muddle through."

He bade me good-by in Trafalgar Square, saying that he must at once seek out the father and brother of the late captain, and tell them the news--that their kinsman was really loyal to his country.

"It will come to them as a ray of light in the dark--

my news," he said. "And now, thank you once again."

We parted and I came back here to my lodgings. The mystery is finally solved, though in such a way it is difficult to believe that it was anything but a nightmare at any time. But solved none the less; and I should be at peace, except for one great black fact that haunts me, will not let me rest. I must tell you, dear lady --And yet I fear it means the end of everything. If only I can make you understand!

I have walked my floor, deep in thought, in puzzlement, in indecision. Now I have made up my mind. There is no other way --I must tell you the truth.

Despite the fact that Bray was Von der Herts; despite the fact that he killed himself at the discovery--despite this and that, and everything-- Bray did not kill Captain Fraser-Freer!

On last Thursday evening, at a little after seven o'clock, I myself climbed the stairs, entered the captain's rooms, picked up that knife from his desk, and stabbed him just above the heart!

What provocation I was under, what stern necessity moved me--all this you must wait until to-morrow to know. I shall spend another anxious day preparing my defense, hoping that through some miracle of mercy you may forgive me--understand that there was nothing else I could do.

Do not judge, dear lady, until you know everything-

-until all my evidence is in your lovely hands.
YOURS, IN ALL HUMILITY.

The first few paragraphs of this the sixth and next to the last letter from the Agony Column man had brought a smile of relief to the face of the girl who read. She was decidedly glad to learn that her friend no longer languished back of those gray walls on Victoria Embankment. With excitement that increased as she went along, she followed Colonel Hughes as--in the letter--he moved nearer and nearer his denouement, until finally his finger pointed to Inspector Bray sitting guilty in his chair. This was an eminently satisfactory solution, and it served the inspector right for locking up her friend. Then, with the suddenness of a bomb from a Zeppelin, came, at the end, her strawberry man's confession of guilt. He was the murderer, after all! He admitted it! She could scarcely believe her eyes.

Yet there it was, in ink as violet as those eyes, on the note paper that had become so familiar to her during the thrilling week just past. She read it a second time, and yet a third. Her amazement gave way to anger; her cheeks flamed. Still--he had asked her not to judge until all his evidence was in. This was a reasonable request surely, and she could not in fairness refuse to grant it.

CHAPTER VIII

So began an anxious day, not only for the girl from

Texas but for all London as well. Her father was bursting with new diplomatic secrets recently extracted from his bootblack adviser. Later, in Washington, he was destined to be a marked man because of his grasp of the situation abroad. No one suspected the bootblack, the power behind the throne; but the gentleman from Texas was destined to think of that able diplomat many times, and to wish that he still had him at his feet to advise him.

"War by midnight, sure!" he proclaimed on the morning of this fateful Tuesday. "I tell you, Marian, we're lucky to have our tickets on the Saronia. Five thousand dollars wouldn't buy them from me to-day! I'll be a happy man when we go aboard that liner day after to-morrow."

Day after to-morrow! The girl wondered. At any rate, she would have that last letter then--the letter that was to contain whatever defense her young friend could offer to explain his dastardly act. She waited eagerly for that final epistle.

The day dragged on, bringing at its close England's entrance into the war; and the Carlton bootblack was a prophet not without honor in a certain Texas heart. And on the following morning there arrived a letter which was torn open by eager trembling fingers. The letter spoke:

DEAR LADY JUDGE: This is by far the hardest to write of all the letters you have had from me. For twenty-four hours I have been planning it. Last night I walked on the Embankment while the hansoms jogged by and the lights of the tramcars danced on Westminster Bridge just as the fireflies used to in the garden back of our house in Kansas. While I walked I planned. To-day, shut up in my rooms, I was also planning. And yet now, when I sit down to write, I am still confused; still at a loss where to begin and what to say, once I have begun.

At the close of my last letter I confessed to you that it was I who murdered Captain Fraser-Freer. That is the truth. Soften the blow as I may, it all comes down to that. The bitter truth!

Not a week ago--last Thursday night at seven--I climbed our dark stairs and plunged a knife into the heart of that defenseless gentleman. If only I could point out to you that he had offended me in some way; if I could prove to you that his death was necessary to me, as it really was to Inspector Bray-- then there might be some hope of your ultimate pardon. But, alas! he had been most kind to me-- kinder than I have allowed you to guess from my letters. There was no actual need to do away with him. Where shall I look for a defense?

At the moment the only defense I can think of is simply this--the captain knows I killed him!

Even as I write this, I hear his footsteps above me, as I heard them when I sat here composing my first letter to you. He is dressing for dinner. We are to dine together at Romano's.

And there, my lady, you have finally the answer to the mystery that has--I hope--puzzled you. I killed my friend the captain in my second letter to you, and all the odd developments that followed lived only in my imagination as I sat here beside the green-shaded lamp in my study, plotting how I should write seven letters to you that would, as the novel advertisements say, grip your attention to the very end. Oh, I am guilty--there is no denying that. And, though I do not wish to ape old Adam and imply that I was tempted by a lovely woman, a strict regard for the truth forces me to add that there is also guilt upon your head. How so? Go back to that message you inserted in the Daily Mail: "The grapefruit lady's great fondness for mystery and romance--"

You did not know it, of course; but in those words you passed me a challenge I could not resist; for making plots is the business of life--more, the breath of life--to me. I have made many; and perhaps you have followed some of them, on Broadway. Perhaps you have seen a play of mine announced for early production in London. There was mention of it in the program at the Palace. That was the business which kept me in England. The project has been abandoned now and I am free to go back home.

Thus you see that when you granted me the privilege of those seven letters you played into my hands. So, said I, she longs for mystery and romance. Then, by the Lord Harry, she shall have them!

And it was the tramp of Captain Fraser-Freer's boots above my head that showed me the way. A fine, stalwart, cordial fellow--the captain--who has been very kind to me since I presented my letter of introduction from his cousin, Archibald Enwright. Poor Archie! A meek, correct little soul, who would be horrified beyond expression if he knew that of him I had made a spy and a frequenter of Limehouse!

The dim beginnings of the plot were in my mind when I wrote that first letter, suggesting that all was not regular in the matter of Archie's note of introduction. Before I wrote my second, I knew that nothing but the death of Fraser-Freer would do me. I recalled that Indian knife I had seen upon his desk, and from that moment he was doomed. At that time I had no idea how I should solve the mystery. But I had read and wondered at those four strange messages in the Mail, and I resolved that they must figure in the scheme of things.

The fourth letter presented difficulties until I returned from dinner that night and saw a taxi waiting before our quiet house. Hence the visit of the woman with the lilac perfume. I am afraid the Wilhelmstrasse would have little use for a lady spy who advertised herself in so foolish a manner. Time for writing the fifth letter arrived. I felt that I should now be placed under arrest. I had a faint little hope that you would be sorry about that. Oh, I'm a brute, I know!

Early in the game I had told the captain of the cruel way in which I had disposed of him. He was much amused; but he insisted, absolutely, that he must be vindicated before the close of the series, and I was with him there. He had been so bully about it all. A chance remark of his gave me my solution. He said he had it on good authority that the chief of the Czar's bureau for capturing spies in Russia was himself a spy. And so--why not a spy in Scotland Yard?

I assure you, I am most contrite as I set all this down here. You must remember that when I began my story there was no idea of war. Now all Europe is aflame; and in the face of the great conflict, the awful suffering to come, I and my little plot begin to look--well, I fancy you know just how we look.

Forgive me. I am afraid I can never find the words to tell you how important it seemed to interest you in my letters--to make you feel that I am an entertaining person worthy of your notice. That morning when you entered the Canton breakfast room was really the biggest in my life. I felt as though you had brought with you through that doorway-- But I have no right to say it. I have the right to say nothing save that now--it is all left to you. If I have offended, then I shall never hear from you again.

The captain will be here in a moment. It is near the hour set and he is never late. He is not to return to India, but expects to be drafted for the Expeditionary Force that will be sent to the Continent. I hope the German Army will be kinder to him than I was!

My name is Geoffrey West. I live at nineteen Adelphi Terrace--in rooms that look down on the most wonderful garden in London. That, at least, is real. It is very quiet there to-night, with the city and its continuous hum of war and terror seemingly a million miles away.

Shall we meet at last? The answer rests entirely with you. But, believe me, I shall be anxiously waiting to know; and if you decide to give me a chance to explain--to denounce myself to you in person--then a happy man will say good-by to this garden and these dim dusty rooms and follow you to the ends of the earth--aye, to Texas itself!

Captain Fraser-Freer is coming down the stairs. Is this good-by forever, my lady? With all my soul, I hope not.

YOUR CONTRITE STRAWBERRY MAN.

CHAPTER IX

Words are futile things with which to attempt a description of the feelings of the girl at the Canton as she read this, the last letter of seven written to her through the medium of her maid, Sadie Haight. Turning the pages of the dictionary casually, one might enlist a few--for example, amazement, anger, unbelief, wonder. Perhaps, to go back to the letter a, even amusement. We may leave her with the solution to the puzzle in her hand, the Saronia a little more than a day away, and a weirdly mixed company of emotions struggling in her soul.

And leaving her thus, let us go back to Adelphi Terrace and a young man exceedingly worried.

Once he knew that his letter was delivered, Mr. Geoffrey West took his place most humbly on the anxious seat. There he writhed through the long hours of Wednesday morning. Not to prolong this painful picture, let us hasten to add that at three o'clock that same afternoon came a telegram that was to end suspense. He tore it open and read:

STRAWBERRY MAN: I shall never, never forgive, you. But we are sailing tomorrow on the Saronia. Were you thinking of going home soon? MARIAN A. LARNED.

Thus it happened that, a few minutes later, to the crowd of troubled Americans in a certain steamship booking office there was added a wild-eyed young man who further upset all who saw him. To weary clerks he proclaimed in fiery tones that he must sail on the Saronia. There seemed to be no way of appeasing him. The offer of a private liner would not have interested him.

He raved and tore his hair. He ranted. All to no avail. There was, in plain American, "nothing doing!"

Damp but determined, he sought among the crowd for one who had bookings on the Saronia. He could find, at first, no one so lucky; but finally he ran across Tommy Gray. Gray, an old friend, admitted when pressed that he had a passage on that most desirable boat. But the offer of all the king's horses and all the king's gold left him unmoved. Much, he said, as he would have liked to oblige, he and his wife were determined. They would sail.

It was then that Geoffrey West made a compact with his friend. He secured from him the necessary steamer labels and it was arranged that his baggage was to go aboard the Saronia as the property of Gray.

"But," protested Gray, "even suppose you do put this through; suppose you do manage to sail without a ticket--where will you sleep? In chains somewhere below, I fancy."

"No matter!" bubbled West. "I'll sleep in the dining saloon, in a lifeboat, on the lee scuppers--whatever they are. I'll sleep in the air, without any visible support! I'll sleep anywhere--nowhere --but I'll sail! And as for irons--they don't make 'em strong enough to hold me."

At five o'clock on Thursday afternoon the Saronia slipped smoothly away from a Liverpool dock. Twenty-five hundred Americans--about twice the number the boat could comfortably carry--stood on her decks and cheered. Some of those in that crowd who had millions of money were booked for the steerage. All of them were destined to experience during that crossing hunger, annoyance, discomfort. They were to be stepped on, sat on, crowded and jostled. They suspected as much when the boat left the dock. Yet they cheered!

Gayest among them was Geoffrey West, triumphant

amid the confusion. He was safely aboard; the boat was on its way! Little did it trouble him that he went as a stowaway, since he had no ticket; nothing but an overwhelming determination to be on the good ship Saronia.

That night as the Saronia stole along with all deck lights out and every porthole curtained, West saw on the dim deck the slight figure of a girl who meant much to him. She was standing staring out over the black waters; and, with wildly beating heart, he approached her, not knowing what to say, but feeling that a start must be made somehow.

"Please pardon me for addressing--" he began. "But I want to tell you--"

She turned, startled; and then smiled an odd little smile, which he could not see in the dark.

"I beg your pardon," she said. "I haven't met you, that I recall--"

"I know," he answered. "That's going to be arranged to-morrow. Mrs. Tommy Gray says you crossed with them--"

"Mere steamer acquaintances," the girl replied coldly.

"Of course! But Mrs. Gray is a darling--she'll fix that all right. I just want to say, before to-morrow comes--"

"Wouldn't it be better to wait?"

"I can't! I'm on this ship without a ticket. I've got to go down in a minute and tell the purser that. Maybe he'll throw me overboard; maybe he'll lock me up. I don't know what they do with people like me. Maybe they'll make a stoker of me. And then I shall have to stoke, with no chance of seeing you again. So that's why I want to say now--I'm sorry I have such a keen imagination. It carried me away--really it did! I didn't mean to deceive you with those letters; but, once I got started-- You know, don't you, that I love you with all my heart? From the moment you came into the Canton that morning I--"

"Really--Mr.--Mr.--"

"West--Geoffrey West. I adore you! What can I do to prove it? I'm going to prove it--before this ship docks in the North River. Perhaps I'd better talk to your father, and tell him about the Agony Column and those seven letters--"

"You'd better not! He's in a terribly bad humor. The dinner was awful, and the steward said we'd be looking back to it and calling it a banquet before the voyage ends. Then, too, poor dad says he simply can not sleep in the stateroom they've given him--"

"All the better! I'll see him at once. If he stands for me now he'll stand for me any time! And, before I go down and beard a harsh-looking purser in his den, won't you believe me when I say I'm deeply in love--"

"In love with mystery and romance! In love with your own remarkable powers of invention! Really, I can't take you seriously--"

"Before this voyage is ended you'll have to. I'll prove to you that I care. If the purser lets me go free--"

"You have much to prove," the girl smiled. "To-morrow--when Mrs. Tommy Gray introduces us--I may accept you--as a builder of plots. I happen to know you are good. But--as-- It's too silly! Better go and have it out with that purser."

Reluctantly he went. In five minutes he was back. The girl was still standing by the rail.

"It's all right!" West said. "I thought I was doing something original, but there were eleven other people in the same fix. One of them is a billionaire from Wall Street. The purser collected some money from us and told us to sleep on the deck--if we could find room."

"I'm sorry," said the girl. "I rather fancied you in the role of stoker." She glanced about her at the dim deck. "Isn't this exciting? I'm sure this voyage is going to be filled with mystery and romance."

"I know it will be full of romance," West answered. "And the mystery will be--can I convince you--"

"Hush!" broke in the girl. "Here comes father! I shall be very happy to meet you--to-morrow. Poor dad! he's looking for a place to sleep."

Five days later poor dad, having slept each night on deck in his clothes while the ship plowed through a cold drizzle, and having starved in a sadly depleted dining saloon, was a sight to move the heart of a political opponent. Immediately after a dinner that had scarcely satisfied a healthy Texas appetite he lounged gloomily in the deck chair which was now his stateroom. Jauntily Geoffrey West came and sat at his side.

"Mr. Larned," he said, "I've got something for you."

And, with a kindly smile, he took from his pocket and handed over a large, warm baked potato. The Texan eagerly accepted the gift.

"Where'd you get it?" he demanded, breaking open his treasure.

"That's a secret," West answered. "But I can get as many as I want. Mr. Larned, I can say this--you will not go hungry any longer. And there's something else I ought to speak of. I am sort of aiming to marry your daughter."

Deep in his potato the Congressman spoke:

"What does she say about it?"

"Oh, she says there isn't a chance. But--"

"Then look out, my boy! She's made up her mind to have you."

"I'm glad to hear you say that. I really ought to tell you who I am. Also, I want you to know that, before your daughter and I met, I wrote her seven letters--"

"One minute," broke in the Texan. "Before you go into all that, won't you be a good fellow and tell me where you got this potato?"

West nodded.

"Sure!" he said; and, leaning over, he whispered.

For the first time in days a smile appeared on the face of the older man.

"My boy," he said, "I feel I'm going to like you. Never mind the rest. I heard all about you from your friend Gray; and as for those letters--they were the only thing that made the first part of this trip bearable. Marian gave them to me to read the night we came on board."

Suddenly from out of the clouds a long-lost moon appeared, and bathed that over-crowded ocean liner in a flood of silver. West left the old man to his potato and went to find the daughter.

She was standing in the moonlight by the rail of the forward deck, her eyes staring dreamily ahead toward the great country that had sent her forth light-heartedly for to adventure and to see. She turned as West came up.

"I have just been talking with your father," he said.

"He tells me he thinks you mean to take me, after all." She laughed.

"To-morrow night," she answered, "will be our last on board. I shall give you my final decision then."

"But that is twenty-four hours away! Must I wait so long as that?"

"A little suspense won't hurt you. I can't forget those long days when I waited for your letters--"

"I know! But can't you give me--just a little hint--here --to-night?"

"I am without mercy--absolutely without mercy!"

And then, as West's fingers closed over her hand, she added softly: "Not even the suspicion of a hint, my dear--except to tell you that--my answer will be--yes."

Made in the USA
Monee, IL
07 February 2023